Intuition

Kate Allenton

Copyright © 2012 Kate Allenton

All rights reserved.

ISBN: 0615614671

ISBN-13: 9780615614670

Intuition

Published by Coastal Escape Publishing

DEDICATION

This is dedicated to my daughter,
Taylor,
Think big, the possibilities are endless.
Happy Birthday.

And

To my son, Thomas,
You can be anything you want to be.
Congrats on graduating.

And

To my dad,
I miss you more than words can say.

ACKNOWLEDGMENTS

I want to thank, my family for their patience. Without them, I would have never finished the rough draft.

My mom, who will always be my biggest fan.

My awesome sister, Vicki, for being on the cover of Touch of Fate- Book 2 in the Bennett Sister Series.

Jeannie, if it hadn't been for you dragging me to see a Vampire movie of all things, I would have never started reading the sequels, which in turn lead me to my writing.

Lisa, may we grow older than any speed limit sign and always remain friends.

All of my critique partners, you rock.

All of my friends for their valuable input, especially Carol, for insisting my heroine be true to herself.

To my co-workers, who had to listen to every detail about this book on more than one occasion, especially you Sherri.

And a special shout out to Kate Freiman for bringing some structure to my book.

CHAPTER 1

Out of all the unique gifts she and her siblings had inherited, one of Emma Bennett's was the ability to see the dead. Not all dead people, just one in particular: a stubborn, old, crazy woman who wouldn't go away. The old spirit was just one of her many secrets. Heck, each member of her family had at least one of their own to deal with, some worse than hers, so she wouldn't complain.

Emma glanced at the clock and jumped to her feet. "Abby's going to kill me for making her wait." She shoved her supply order into her desk drawer. Family dinners were her only chance to be herself with no worries about the oddities surrounding her life.

A chill skirted across her arms, making the little hairs stand up, announcing Momma

Mae's ghostly presence before she materialized in the micro-suede brown chair across from her desk. "You're never on time, Emma. It's a wonder destiny hasn't passed you by."

Though Emma was the only one able to see Momma Mae, the ghost was as real to her as any other person in her life—a part of her family that seemed here to stay, no matter how many times Emma wished her away and chanted "Just go toward the light."

Momma Mae's spirit had shown herself for the first time thirty years before when Emma had almost drown, and she didn't seem to be leaving any time soon. The ghost looked in her early seventies. She had an even laid-back temperament and did nothing but talk in riddles. Emma had quit trying to make sense of her gibberish a long time ago.

"Why don't you tell me what the future holds?" Emma asked while rolling her eyes. "Then I'll decide if I'd rather just skip it." She gave a lopsided smile before grabbing her black leather purse and maneuvering through her now-crowded office stuffed with furniture she'd ordered from the Internet.

"Your future doesn't include that young man you were dating. I can tell you that much."

Hell, that was a no-brainer. "I sort of figured that one out on my own, Momma

Mae, when I caught the bastard cheating on me."

Her last boyfriend, Ben Johnson, had lasted for three months. Emma didn't love him, but she couldn't have predicted that he was a cheater. She'd met him at one of her sister's fundraisers. A prominent attorney in town, handsome, and attentive, she'd decided to take a chance on him and got burned by his deceit.

She tripped over the gaudy couch, hitting her shin. "That's going to leave a bruise," Emma mumbled while bent over rubbing the sore spot. She let out a heavy sigh of resignation and narrowed her eyes at the large couch. *It looked better in the catalog.*

The back of the café was usually her quiet place, her own personal space, to be alone and free to be herself, flaws and all. Well, today was anything but ordinary. The constant, loud beeping from the construction equipment in the parking lot and the jackhammers chipping away at the concrete behind the café made her head throb. The muscles in her shoulders had tensed when she tried to concentrate on the report she'd read several times and still didn't understand. *Where's a pair of earplugs when you need them?*

Overnight, her quiet Zen-like place had turned into her own personal hell, and they didn't seem to be stopping anytime soon. She wished they were already done; not only did the awful noise cut her work production in half, it nixed her ability to slide out the back door undetected.

The café brimmed with people of all ages tonight. The earthy décor and dimmed lights added to the quiet ambiance, a place to relax and unwind. The Starlight Café was her baby. Her only dream that had come true. There was no way she'd make it to the front door without being stopped. She never could. It wasn't her staff that stopped her; they were competent enough to run the café. It was her patrons that seemed to crave her attention.

The little town of Southall, North Carolina seemed to have a magnetic pull against the residents, not letting anyone escape from its grips. Those that grew up here stayed while any new visitors always seemed to leave. Emma had spent her thirty-five plus years growing up in this town and getting to know most of the people in it. Like most small towns, it thrived on juicy gossip. It was only a matter of time before the gossip mill got wind of her and Ben's fiasco.

Gone were the quiet days when she'd greeted her customers with a smile and friendly hello. Her life seemed more hectic than before, a price she gladly paid for ultimately fulfilling her dream of opening the café. The support from the town and her inheritance had made her dream become a reality. The hefty sum of money had done the job, allowing her to put all of her focus into the café and live comfortably off the rest. After the death of their parents, the same community had opened their arms to the Bennett children and embraced each one in their own way.

Some of her other dreams would always be out of reach no matter how many countless stars in the night sky she wished on or how much she had in her bank account. Money wasn't going to buy her the one thing she craved the most. True love.

It's going to be a busy night.

With her head down and hand stuck in her bag, digging for her elusive car keys, Emma bounced off of what felt like a solid brick wall. She shifted her weight and regained her footing before she ended on her butt. The contents of her purse, however, weren't as lucky. Everything scattered across the floor at her feet. *Crap.* She let out a long exhale and shook her head as she squatted to pick up her things, pausing at the sight of some huge, dusty brown hiking boots.

Her gaze traveled up the mountain of a man, to find muscular thighs encased in blue jeans that hung loose on his hips. A dark-blue t-shirt displaying the words *Tactical Maneuvers* outlined his broad chest and muscular arms.

"Yeah, right," she whispered. *If he possessed any tactical maneuvers, he could have at least gotten out of the way.* Her upward glance stopped on his handsome face, unfamiliar but damned sexy. With high cheekbones, stubborn jaw, and firm sensual lips that begged to be kissed, this guy had it all, the complete package set off by his striking blue eyes. The color reminded her of the ocean.

Christmas had come early. He would look scrumptious under her tree in nothing but an oversized red bow. Emma settled her gaze on his handsome face. She could feel the heat traveling to her cheeks. She cleared her throat and was glad he hadn't heard her comment. It wasn't this stranger's fault. No, this gorgeous man could delay her any day of the week, and she wouldn't complain. "I'm so sorry."

The man chuckled; his lips tilted in a bemused smile as he leaned over and offered her a hand. "No worries, angel. You didn't hurt me."

Aw hell, even his deep voice oozed of sex. Heat crept into Emma's cheeks as she stood. "I'm late for a meeting and wasn't paying attention. It was all my fault. Sorry about that." She walked to an empty table and placed her purse on it, shoving her things inside. His fingers brushed hers as he handed her the lipstick that had rolled by his large brown boots. The light touch sent tingles up her arm, causing an instant shiver to course through her body. She inhaled; his earthy fragrance tickled her nose. *Yep, just what I thought... He's all man, one-hundred percent prime grade A beef. No need for fries or condiments. He's all the meal a woman would want.*

"It was just an accident. Really, I'm fine."

"Have a seat," she said, motioning to one of her staff. "Mister . . ." She bit her bottom lip and raised an eyebrow awaiting his reply. His dimples almost melted her on the spot.

"Jake."

Emma turned and spoke to her server. "Helen, Jake's meals are on the house, for him and his guest." She scanned the dining room, trying to figure out which beautiful woman might be with the stranger tonight. The gazes of several attractive women traveled the length of his body, the women smiling at what they saw. She hadn't been the only one affected by his handsome, rugged good looks. So which one would it be? The blonde walking in their direction or the redhead coming through the door? Obviously, all he had to do was take his pick.

Jake cleared his throat, drawing her attention from the women's blatant perusal of their new prey. "Party of one…unless you'd care to join me?"

Emma's heart skipped a beat. *What I wouldn't give to blow off my sister and spend the night getting to know this man, even if only for one night.* Just as quick as the thought entered her mind, she knew she was kidding herself. Nope, a relationship would never work. The reason appeared beside her, confirming her rationale. *What a shame.*

Momma Mae held her arms crossed over her chest and tapped her white nurse-looking shoes against the mauve carpet.

"Focus, Emma. You need to go meet Abby," the ghost said, vanishing just as quickly as she appeared.

Emma sighed and sagged against the table, reclaiming her composure; she pushed her shoulders back and stood. "I'm sorry; I can't, but please enjoy your dinner."

She threw the purse strap over her shoulder as she made her way to the door. She could feel his gaze on her, and taking a chance, she glanced back once more at the sexy man. Just what she'd thought; he was watching her walk away. His attention traveled up from her backside to her face, and Emma couldn't help herself. She grinned and winked. He was one more thing to add to her list of regrets, although images of him would star in her dreams for several nights to come.

Emma pushed through the door and stepped into the cooling autumn air. Tonight, even the normally quiet streets seemed bustling with energy, like her café. Kids hanging out on skateboards and couples strolling the streets. Out of the corner of her eye, she thought she saw a shadow move between the buildings, but dismissed it to the setting sun.

She looked across the street at the cherry-red VW she loved so much, but even it didn't lift her spirits like it usually did. Growing up in this small town had always been kind of dull for most of the locals, but the gifts her and her siblings possessed always seemed to keep them entertained.

Before she stepped off the curb, she spotted Vivian, her hairdresser, a miracle with shears. Her natural red curls bounced around her shoulders as she headed Emma's way. Dark sunglasses covered her jade eyes. Vivian called out and scurried up the sidewalk, almost tripping as she glanced over her shoulder. Her black spandex leggings accentuated the bulges her bright-yellow top failed to conceal. The ensemble reminded

Emma of a bumblebee, and the woman was just as noisy, too. No matter how the woman dressed and acted, she was still one of Emma's only friends, and Emma wouldn't change a thing about her eccentric personality. Not counting her sisters, Vivian was her only friend who knew her secret and never judged.

"Hey, Viv," she said.

Just weeks before, Momma Mae pestered the crap out of Emma, insisting she warn Vivian to get away from her abusive boyfriend. She said the asshole had a dark aura, one of the worst kinds she'd ever seen and feared he was going to kill Vivian. It was so out of character for Momma Mae to interfere with fate's plan it left Emma with no choice.

Emma hesitated before telling Vivian the truth about Momma Mae and her message, but in the end, her friend's safety won out. It was worth more than any ridicule that would ever be thrown her way. Since she'd discovered her ability all those years ago, Emma adamantly refused to reveal her secret to another soul outside of her family, always keeping people at arm's length, worried they'd think she was a freak as her elementary teacher had.

Vivian stopped in front of Emma and lowered her glasses. "You were right about

Roger." The black eye she sported glistened an ugly shade of green and yellow. "He hit me when I broke things off."

Emma gently squeezed her hand and gave her a sad smile. "I'm so sorry, Viv. Are you okay?"

"I'm terrified! My last nerves are ready to snap. I don't know what hole he might crawl out of next." She wrapped her arms across her waist, and her body slightly shivered. "I'm staying with my sister until the restraining order is issued and he moves out."

Vivian did a slow, deep inhale and exhale, an obvious attempt at calm her nerves. Emma should have thought it odd that she'd never been to Vivian's house since they were friends, but now she understood why.

Emma leaned over, wrapped her arms around her friend, and whispered, "I'm glad you got away from the bastard. You deserve so much better."

Vivian's older sister, Janet, pulled into the empty parking space next to Emma's car and got out. She smiled and waved as she crossed the street in their direction. "Hey, Emma," she said, before turning to her sister. "Viv, sorry I'm late. I lost track of time. Are you ready to eat?"

"I think I need a drink," Vivian mumbled under her breath, glancing up and down the street. Her nervous energy was almost like a living thing rolling off her in waves. Vivian turned to leave, glancing over her shoulder, she shouted, "Don't forget about your hair appointment at the end of the month."

Emma nodded and crossed the street toward her car. Instant headache. *Not again.* The pain hit hard, and the intensity had her gripping the car door for support. She scanned the surrounding area and clenched her jaw.

Trouble is brewing somewhere.

Emma's second gift was one she would gladly give away—her own personal warning system for trouble. Headaches and stomach cramps for most normal women meant PMS; for Emma, they were precursors to dangers that lurked nearby. When Emma was growing up, her family had called it her intuition, but Emma commonly referred to it as a pain in the ass.

And my radar is shining like a beacon tonight.

CHAPTER 2

Ben Johnson stood in the shadows between the two buildings and ran a hand through his hair, watching the exchange between Emma and Vivian. *She ruined everything*. Ben clenched his fist tight, almost breaking his cell phone clutched in his palm. The loan shark's threats for their money were getting worse. If he didn't do something soon, it was just a matter of time before they'd kill him. It was money he didn't have and had no way to obtain. Emma had made sure of that.

His last little Vegas trip had wiped him clean, and now she'd single-handedly ruined his only way out. Emma was going to be his ticket; now he wasn't sure what he was going to do. *The bitch is going to pay.* He wanted to bang his head against the brick building for being so stupid, for screwing the little socialite that had thrown herself at him. Ben hadn't expected Emma to walk into his office while he had the curvy redhead bent over his desk.

Ben punched in numbers on his phone. "I'm watching them now. She's in front of the café about to leave to meet her sister. I'll follow her until you get there. Yeah, you know the place. It never changes."

Ben grunted a few times before adding, "She's talking to Vivian. I'm sure it's all Emma's fault and don't forget you owe me. Your ass would be rotting in jail right now if it hadn't been for me getting those charges dropped so get your ass over there."

A smile formed on his lips as a plan formed in his mind. Emma was going to give him the money one way or the other. Either dead or alive, Emma was his ticket out of this mess, and the best part was, the slime ball would be going down for it. Ben's hands would remain clean.

Intuition

****

Emma's inner danger radar simmered in her gut but never fully left as she and her younger sister, Abby, lingered at Bernie's, letting their food settle. The local Mexican restaurant had been a family favorite since childhood. The familiar aroma of salsa filled the air. The place had aged over the years; the faded red and tan walls had lost their shine years before. The torn vinyl seats of the booths needed replacing, and the menus now had writing on them indicating the changes. Other families sat nearby laughing and talking, oblivious to everyone around. She could remember a time in her life several years before when her family had been the same way. Her heart ached a little bit more each time she came here, remembering the happy times and the sad.

The pain from losing their parents wouldn't stop Emma and her siblings from going there once a month. They all longed for the good memories this place brought back; it offered a little peace in each of their crazy lives.

Once she had asked Momma Mae why she couldn't see her parents, considering her gift. The old lady shook her head and said she wasn't ready yet.

What the hell did the old bat know, anyway?

Like Bernie's, all the surrounding buildings were falling apart. Broken bricks and windows littered the landscape. The fact that the restaurant was still standing and not abandoned like the rest of the buildings amazed her. A talented graffiti artist had expanded his canvas, using neighboring buildings to display his work. This part of the city was a ghost town, if you didn't count the homeless that covered the streets and alleyways. The once thriving community had suffered when the economy had taken a nosedive and people started losing jobs. Emma was blessed her small café was doing so well. It was a shame this neighborhood now stood in ruins, but even the decay of the community wouldn't stop their monthly dinners. The only thing missing tonight was the rest of their siblings.

"Where's Mike?" Emma asked her sister.

"I think he's still at the station." Abby peeled the label off her beer bottle, her lips pulled in a tight line as she sat lost in thought.

Emma had seen that familiar look of concern before. Mike's choice of professions wasn't easy for the Bennett sisters to swallow after their dad's death. The Bennett women had learned the risk involved with having a family member as a cop the hard way, and their dad hadn't been invincible. Not having answers to his unexpected death prevented any of them having closure. Their grief was enough for a lifetime, and Momma Mae was the crutch Emma grabbed hold of for dear life to help her cope with the pain that threatened to consume her.

Momma Mae was a constant pain in the ass, but she had been Emma's only comfort the night her father died. Momma Mae had soothed her through hours of tears, bloodshot eyes, and unanswered prayers. The family had survived, and the pain got less as the years went by, but Emma's heart had never truly healed from the loss and probably never would, not without the answers Mike and the rest of them were desperate to find.

Emma, Abby, and Claire all worried their brother might meet the same fate. A dragon slayer would have been a safer profession than a cop on these streets.

"Claire couldn't make it either. She's having another one of her fundraisers tonight." Emma loved her sister and would paste another fake smile on her face in the name of sisterly love. Fundraisers were

Claire's way of dealing with her loss. She would throw herself into the events one hundred percent and expect the family to play along. If they hadn't been so damned important to Claire, they'd quit showing up.

"I guess she's expecting us to show up?" Abby played with her beer bottle, making rings of condensation on the table and picking at the label.

"I told her I'd be at the cancer benefit at the end of the month. She's already sent over my dress." Emma didn't quite feel the smile that formed on her lips. The benefit was important to all of them, a constant reminder that a cure hadn't existed for their mom. Attending two fundraisers was a lot to ask from someone who felt uncomfortable around the type of guest expected to attend. Avoiding her ex, who ran in the same circles, would be hard enough once a month, much less twice. She guessed it was time to come clean about Ben and tell her siblings why she'd broken it off... Well, it couldn't hurt to wait one more day. *Could it?*

The air around her grew heavy, making it difficult to breathe. The prickly hair on her nape stood on end, and the severity of the cramps fueled her unease. The air suddenly vibrated with energy, bad energy she felt deep down in her bones. Emma grasped the table to root herself in the booth. The need to flee was overwhelming. She glanced around at the patrons sitting close by, looking for a plausible reason for her panic. An older couple holding hands smiled lovingly at each other. A child made silly faces at her parents. An old man sat at the end of the bar, reading a paper and sipping his coffee. Nothing seemed out of place.

Momma Mae appeared beside her and whispered into her ear, "You need to leave now, baby girl."

Abby leaned forward. "What's wrong?"

Emma tried to keep most of it to herself when things were about to happen, but she refused to hide possible danger from her siblings. They had their own gifts to deal with. Like genetics that suggested a big nose in some families, the DNA of her family held a unique and strange code. They all had some craziness to deal with.

"I'm not sure… but it's not good." She dug in her purse for her cell, hit speed dial, and prayed for an answer.

"Hey, Em, what's up?" her brother, Mike, asked.

Emma felt a little of the tension coursing through her shoulders ease when she heard his familiar voice, but it did nothing for the cramps assaulting her midsection.

"My spidey senses are tingling."

"You sure? Or is Momma Mae bored and ready to go?" he asked sarcastically.

"Yeah, I'm positive. Abby and I are at Bernie's. Can you stop by Claire's and check on her? She's having one of her parties and won't hear the phone ring if I try to call." Emma had figured out early on that the feelings didn't necessarily mean the danger was directed at her. Every one of her family members seemed possible targets.

"I'll check on her myself… Em, do you have your gun?"

"I left it in the car. There's nothing suspicious or out of place, but Mike, I'm just not sure." Emma continued scanning the restaurant, experiencing some of the most intense feelings she'd ever had. Her head was pounding, and a shiver ran down her spine. "It's strong this time, and Momma Mae says we need to leave."

"Stay put. I'm sending someone to get you."

The stench of food burning hit her nose moments before the kitchen staff burst through the doors. Emma heard their rapid Spanish but had no idea what it meant. She noticed the smoke billowing out of the kitchen only seconds before the alarm blared throughout the building. *This can't be good.*

The alarm intensified the pain. Her head felt ready to explode, and now a ringing erupted in her ears.

"Call the fire department! The kitchen's on fire!" she yelled into her phone before she flipped it shut. Budding fear crept up her spine like the rising smoke coming through the kitchen door. Emma rushed to her feet, throwing her purse strap across her body, and pulled Abby from the booth, bumping into the old man running for the closest exit. Children cried as their parents snatched them from the tables and ran for the door.

"We need to get out!" she screamed over the loud noises.

The exits were the first thing Emma noticed when entering any building. Growing up in a family full of cops had its benefits. She knew her surroundings, the exits, the people, and cars in the parking lot. The games they'd played as children would pay off today. Emma jerked to a halt when she noticed a large man blocking the exit closest to their table. He was dressed in black with his massive arms crossed over his chest. A sinister smile etched in the lines across his face. Fear crept up Emma's spine and had her backtracking for the front doors instead.

She inhaled, and smoke filled her lungs, burning and making her cough. She lowered to a crouch to avoid the gray smoke enveloping most of the restaurant and making it difficult to see. Emma scurried to the front doors with a firm grip on Abby's hand. The snapping of the fire echoed in her ears as she pushed open the door. The night air echoed with sirens in the distance. Help was on the way.

The staff and patrons from the restaurant stood on the cracked sidewalk watching in disbelief. People around them were coughing and dazed, trying to make sense out of what had started as a normal night. The ones with children had a death grip on their kids' hands, either afraid they'd run off or thankful they were still alive; Emma didn't know which. Probably both.

The raging fire illuminated the night sky and surrounding area with an eerie reddish-orange glow. The heat from the towering inferno made her exposed flesh feel sunburned. Come morning, the last tie to her parents would be nothing but ash.

Emma's car was parked closest to the street entrance for an easy exit. Who knew it would be the safest place in the lot from the fire raging in the night sky? Emma grabbed Abby's hand and started to pull her toward the car. Another sudden jolt of pain had her doubled over, clutching her head in a feeble attempt to stop what felt like a million needles stabbing her temples.

This is so not happening.

Abby grabbed Emma's arm to keep her from collapsing. "Doesn't the pain ease up after the disaster?" she whispered in Emma's ear.

"It must not be over." She guided Abby farther away from the building and patrons to create a safer distance, not knowing what other danger to expect. The same freakishly large man who'd blocked their exit only minutes before now prowled closer with the same evil grin. The glint on the eight-inch silver blade clenched in his hand drew her attention, making another shiver race down her spin. It didn't take her intuition to realize this man was dangerous; his aura oozed with it.

Emma whispered to Abby, not taking her eyes from the man's approach. "Do you have your gun?"

Abby turned to see what had Emma enthralled and gulped before she patted the back waist of her jeans. "No."

"Damn, this just keeps getting better and better." Emma stood to her full height, ignoring the pains racking her body. The seconds of his approach seemed like hours as her mind contemplated what this asshole might want.

The stranger narrowed his black eyes and let out a low laugh at the same moment Mamma Mae screamed, "Run, baby girl!"

CHAPTER 3

"Run, Abby!" Emma screamed as she sidestepped the crazy knife-wielding hulk of a man.

His erratic swing sliced the air, making her jump back and missing her by several inches. She countered with a kick to his balls. His hand cupped his groin as his enormous body doubled over. Emma dropped and circled with her leg extended to sweep his feet and drop his unusually large frame on his ass, giving Emma and Abby a much-needed head start.

Abby stood frozen in place, her eyes widened in fear with her mouth hanging open. Emma tugged Abby's hand, determined to get her to safety, and cursed herself for leaving her gun in the car. She had to rely on her quick thinking if they were going to get out of this mess.

Her dad's voice echoed in her mind, *Keep them safe.* Emma's father believed in intuition and frequently lectured them on listening to their guts, pounding it in their heads when they were little so it would come as second nature. And right now, hers was screaming to run like hell.

They ran toward her car, not waiting around for another slice.

"Damn, I need a keyless entry."

One click of a button would have given them a barrier from the maniac and a chance to escape. She cursed her thrifty self for not indulging in the extra for her car. She glanced back over her shoulder; he wasn't far behind. Unable to unlock it in time, she kept running, dragging her sister behind her, hoping she would snap out of the shock.

Abby worked as a forensic investigator, but that didn't mean she had field experience escaping the assholes she used her mind to try to catch. Everyone's attention was drawn to the fire. Not a soul witnessed them running for their lives from this weirdo. The glassy look on Abby's face told Emma she was going to have to get them out of this jam. She had no intention of losing any vital organs to this asshole tonight; he would have to catch them first.

The man charged after them, his bulky, steroid-induced size controlling his pace. His slow movements increased Emma's chance to ditch this creep. Emma and Abby passed an abandoned warehouse, where a dirty man squatted in the alley by his cardboard tent and a bag lady was pushing her shopping cart. At a full-out run, Emma tried to maneuver the corner of the next alley and slammed into the crumbling red brick wall, sending debris raining down on her head.

Unable to stop, Abby bounced off her back forcing what little air Emma had left in her lungs out with a swoosh. Though scratched and bruised, she wasn't stopping. She couldn't afford to. She ran faster down the alley. The adrenaline coursed through her veins, helping to minimize the pain in her limbs.

Her heart was racing, ready to leap out of her chest. She looked back over her shoulder and watched the psycho hit the same wall and land on his ass. Another few seconds added to their lead might just make the difference. The next street held more rundown buildings and not a soul in sight. Even the homeless kept off this street. Her scream for help would go unanswered and their deaths possibly unnoticed for a very long time.

Emma refused to become a morning headline. No way in hell would she let her family suffer another loss, not as long as she was still breathing. She could outsmart this guy if she had time to think, but time wasn't a luxury she had. Determined to get them off the street and out of sight, she shoved open the door of the next building she came to. *Thank god.*

She slammed the door closed and flicked the lock, hoping it would add precious minutes to their escape. Abby and Emma bent over with hands on their knees trying to catch their breath. Emma closed her eyes and clenched her fists before she stood up again. "Who the hell is this guy?"

"I haven't seen him before." Abby lifted from her bent position and locked eyes with Emma. "What are we going to do?"

"Let's see if there's a way out. We need to put more distance between us and this asshole."

Like everything else in the neighborhood, the three-story building was empty and abandoned. She took in a deep breath. The stench of urine and mildew assaulted her nose, almost making her gag. Emma swiped at the beads of sweat trickling down her face.

She hadn't recognized the man chasing them. If he caught them, they didn't stand a chance of overpowering him, but in the fifty-yard dash, he would lose, and that was what she was betting on. It wouldn't take him long to find them, though. They needed to keep going. Emma grabbed Abby's hand in a crushing grip, pulling her toward the rear entrance. She gripped the handle, shaking it with all her strength, then slammed her body into it; the sucker didn't budge.

"Shit!" she screamed, and spun around on her heels looking for another exit. Rust and angry red marks covered her palms from her struggle with the door. She wiped her hands on her jeans and darted for the stairs. The only option was up.

"Who the hell did you piss off?" Abby shouted as she narrowed her blue eyes. Abby was gifted with more than psychometry; she had some serious attitude too. Why couldn't one of them have been gifted with a superpower instead? Superhuman strength or flying would have helped them better then seeing the dead, cramps when danger lurked, and Abby's gift of touching objects and getting feelings and images. If Emma had her vote, she would have picked some bionic abilities or, at the very least, the ability to kick some ass.

"Hell if I know!"

They reached the top of the third flight of stairs in time to hear the sound of wood splintering as the door broke below. Emma's heart pounded against her ribcage. Her lungs burned from lack of oxygen. Frantic now that he had found them, they needed to get out.

"I'm gonna kill you, bitch!"

Her hand flew over her mouth, covering a scream that threatened to erupt. *Who the hell is this guy and what is his problem?* They walked silently and fast. The office on the third floor could hide them for a few minutes, but they would be sitting ducks if found, and it wasn't a gamble she was willing to take. Emma had to keep them moving; they needed to find a way out.

"Come on," Emma whispered, not wanting to give away their position. It wouldn't take him long to notice they weren't on the bottom floor. She heard a curse as their unknown assailant grunted, struggling with the same door they'd been at only minutes before.

Emma prayed there wasn't an alarm and slowly pushed the emergency door to the open roof. Her silent victory was short lived. She knew what they needed and had to find it before he found them.

In her frantic search of the rooftop, she spotted the corroded metal stairs hung over the side of the building. *Freedom.* Crumbled bricks from the deteriorating building lay scattered across the roof. Abby tripped and fell to her knees, taking Emma down with her, adding more cuts to her already battered body. Regaining her balance, she pushed herself up and yanked Abby's arm. Emma whispered in her ear, afraid of being overheard. "Be careful."

Her sister narrowed her eyes, and a frown marred her lips, but she kept going without a sarcastic comment.

Emma glanced over the side of the building and said a silent prayer the stairs were still in one piece and would hold under their combined weight. First Abby and then Emma threw their legs over the side of the building and quickened the pace down the corroded ladder. Almost to the bottom, in her haste, she barely missed crushing Abby's fingers with her foot.

"Watch it."

The three-foot jump from the last rung sent a jarring stab of pain through her tired legs, but it didn't stop her from moving. They needed to get to her car. Sirens in the distance stopped her in mid-dash. *Protection.* She switched direction with new intent.

Rounding the corner to the next street, she jerked Abby to a stop. The familiar red and blue lights from her childhood colored the moonlight. The welcome sight meant they would be safe at last. A renewed shot of adrenaline pumped through her veins.

The slight curve of Abby's lips indicated she'd thought the same thing as well. *Almost there.* She started to sprint and glanced back at Abby, making sure she was keeping up. Emma's body slammed into something hard for the second time that night. The muscular man had appeared out of nowhere. His steel arms circled her, pulling her body tight to his stone chest before she fell. She looked up and into the eyes of the same man from her café.

Not a uniform. Damn. Unsure of his intent and why he was here, she swung a solid right hook hitting him squarely on his jaw. His head barely moved, and his grip tightened. He wouldn't let go even as she squirmed to get out of his arms, pushing hard against his chest. Seconds before she

Intuition - 33 -

was about to lift her knee to make contact with his precious jewels, Momma Mae appeared.

"Good guy, baby girl," Momma Mae whispered in her ear.

Her lips parted as she stood on shaky legs, digesting the old woman's words. She locked her knees to regain her stance. He kept his crushing grip on her arms, making sure she didn't fall to the ground.

"Help us," she begged as she struggled to breathe.

"Slow down. Tell me what's going on." His eyebrows scrunched together.

"A man…" Abby choked out while doubled over, trying to catch her breath.

"With a knife is chasing us," Emma finished as she exhaled her next breath. She glanced over her shoulder and scanned the darkness in search of the deranged man. The embrace of the stranger's arms held her body pressed to his. She shivered, still attempting to push away.

"You must be Emma and Abby. You were supposed to stay put at the restaurant. When I found the car Mike described still in the parking lot and the two of you nowhere in sight, I came looking for you." His smile widened, showing his perfect white teeth and the dimple she'd seen before.

Who is this guy? Emma glanced at Abby with a raised brow. His firm, deep voice commanded her attention. Emma wondered if he'd have the same presence in the sack. What his strong hands would feel like against her naked flesh. *I've got to get a life."*

Emma shook her head to clear her wondering thoughts. She needed to focus on their danger, not the man whose hands held her captive. What did she genuinely know about this guy besides the affect he had on her body? Absolutely nothing.

He suddenly eased his grip and replied. "I'm Jake Donavan. Mike sent me to get you; we need to get in the car." He tilted his head toward the black Mustang. His glance around the area didn't go unnoticed, at least not by a cop's kid. The hairs at the nape of her neck stood up, and a chill traveled down her spine, making her shiver.

"Are you serious? A man is chasing us with a freakin' knife! We don't even know you… you could be with the lunatic." Emma stepped back out of his reach, glad he had let her go and her head had cleared from the sexual haze. She grabbed her cell from her pocket and dialed. Her brother answered on the first ring.

"You all right?"

"Alive," she replied, and cut him off before another question passed his lips.

"Who did you send?" Emma looked over to their potential savior, forming a plan in her head should they need to escape.

"Jake, an old military buddy. Did he find you?"

"Yeah." She released a breath she hadn't realized she was holding and smiled at Momma Mae standing next to Jake. "We're on our way." Emma flipped her phone closed.

His gaze scanned her body. She assumed he was taking inventory of any physical damage. Either that or he worried their bleeding wounds might ruin his car. They were alive, and that was all that mattered. Emma looked down at her grimy and dirty clothes and grimaced.

Abby put her hand on Emma's elbow, steering her to the car. "Come on, Emma, let's go. I'll feel better when we get out of here."

Emma sized Jake up. He looked even more intimidating on the dark street, rugged with a five o'clock shadow she hadn't noticed at the café. A light jacket covered the muscles she had firsthand knowledge that he possessed. They looked to be from hard work in the gym, probably not from a needle puncture like the psycho's.

He could easily take on the lunatic determined to kill them, or at least match him in a fight. Was it coincidence she'd now had two "episodes" when he was around? That was something she would consider, after her baby sister was safe. First running into him in the café and now on the streets, he must have thought she was off her rocker, or at least clumsy as hell.

Her stomach cramps still lingered. She knew the fiend with the onyx eyes lurked just out of sight watching them from deep within the shadows hidden by the night sky. She scanned the area again, but there was still no sign of their attacker. She shivered. They were still in danger and needed to leave, and quick.

"You know where you're going?" Emma asked as she and Abby followed him to the car parked at the curb.

"215 Heritage."

She blew out a breath, and the tension slightly eased from her straining muscles. They couldn't get there fast enough to suit Emma. Jake grabbed the door handle and pulled; the swift movement shifted his jacket, revealing the semi-automatic resting in the holster. She almost missed it. His gaze caught what she was staring at, and he pulled his light jacket tighter to his chest, concealing the weapon from her sight.

Glock. She hoped he knew how to use it, but if he didn't, she sure as hell did.

CHAPTER 4

On the drive to her sister's, Emma watched out the passenger window as they passed the scenery, her mind replaying the chase over and over. She was almost certain she had never seen the knife-wielding giant before. Her gaze turned to the man beside her. His muscular body appeared cramped behind the wheel.

Must not be his car, she thought to herself as she sneaked peeks at him under her lowered eyelashes. His light jacket semi-covered the same blue cotton t-shirt stretched tight across his body at the café. His attempt to hide his bulging muscles was about as effective as the jacket hiding his gun. Neither was working for him. There was nothing sexual about his last embrace, but she couldn't control her body's response to his touch. She remembered everything about him from the café. His touch had turned her insides to mush. Now that the chase was over and the adrenaline coursing through her veins had slowed, she noticed the betrayal of her body. Emma rubbed her arms as an attempt to regain control.

Jake cleared his throat, his deep voice interrupting her perusal of his body. "Are you cold?" Jake asked as he reached for the air conditioner knob.

Emma looked up to his face. She swallowed the lump stuck in her throat and shook her head. "No."

His lips turned up at the edges as he managed a slow smile. Reaching over, he rubbed her leg. His innocent gesture meant to reassure her she was safe, but it only ended up fueling the fire he ignited in her body.

The danger they had been in should have dampened her response to him, but it hadn't. She shifted her gaze back to his face. The reflected light glimmered from the passing cars, highlighting his curly brown hair and setting off his ocean blue eyes. She could get lost looking into those eyes and was sure many women had.

Now that he'd offered her comfort, he was back to business—whatever that was. He pulled his hand back and gripped the wheel; his lips pulled in a tight line. Was he aggravated that he'd had to pick them up or was he worried for them? Jake repeatedly glanced in the rearview mirror, either checking out Abby or looking for a tail. She wasn't sure which, but it was enough to pull her from the spell she had fallen under. A twinge of jealousy hit, and she returned her gaze to the window.

When they arrived at Claire's house, the lengthy rows of limousines and cars had Emma fidgeting in her seat. The disturbing dash from the bald giant had made Emma entirely forget the party in full swing. The overflowing circular drive with expensive cars brought her back to reality. Men in tuxedos lingered on the steps, smoking cigars while talking business. Claire's elegant mansion held a full house tonight, packed with filthy rich and famous people who supported her latest worthwhile cause. Heat traveled into Emma's cheeks when she remembered she looked like hell. Her mussed hair and dirty clothes would be an eyesore for Claire's guests and an embarrassment for her sister. She headed to the kitchen entrance, passing the catering staff as they scurried around, hoping not to embarrass her sister.

They made their way into the study without incident. Jake's hand at the small of Emma's back sent an electrical current tingling through her body. She hadn't remembered her body reacting like this when Ben touched her, hell any of her exes for that matter. God, she hoped the bastard wasn't here. She'd had enough excitement for one night.

Mike paced in front of the stone fireplace, where a warm fire cast its glow over the room. He was wearing a path in Claire's carpet as he kept his gaze down at his feet, his hands fisted at his side. Claire sat behind her mahogany desk, pushing papers around. Her relaxed posture didn't hide the lines that creased her brow, telling Emma her sister was worried. The spacious room was comfortable enough with the supple brown leather sofa and chairs inviting guests to relax. Emma loved this room and often hid here when she had to attend Claire's parties. Mahogany bookshelves lined the room and reached the ceiling. Emma smiled, remembering the endless supply of entertainment she'd found on nights when she should have been mingling with guests. The room was a reader's dream and at times Emma's only escape.

Jake's gentle caress on her lower back pulled her from her memories. She looked up and smiled.

Mike stopped pacing when he noticed their arrival.

"About damn time." Mike's clipped tone reinforced his agitation. He stomped over to Emma and Abby and grabbed them up in a bone-crushing hug that made Emma wince. Soreness had already settled into her bones from their escapades.

The appreciative nod to Jake Donavan didn't go unnoticed. "Thanks for your help."

"You're welcome," Jake replied with an identical nod.

"Em, I thought I told you to stay put. When Jake called saying you two weren't there, you scared the hell out of me."

"That was the plan, big brother, until the knife-carrying, bald giant showed up trying to filet us. My intuition told me to run, so we did."

"The same intuition you had at the restaurant?"

"Is there any other?" Emma ignored the strange looks Jake was giving them as her brother talked in code. She could almost see the wheels spinning as he looked between her and Mike, obviously confused by their conversation.

"Abby, why don't you go get changed for the party and call John while I take Mr. Donavan to the kitchen for a drink?" Claire dutifully said as she held Jake's elbow, guiding him to the door. Claire smiled and winked at Emma as she passed. "We'll talk later."

Abby rushed from the room in a hurry to call John, concern etched on her face. Her son was her life, her top priority.

"Okay, Em, who was chasing you?" Mike asked as he pulled her toward the nearby couch.

"I don't know who he was. It was probably a random attack. He didn't even look familiar." Emma shrugged as she replayed the chase again in her mind.

Letting out a deep sigh and sinking into the couch, she grabbed Mike's hand. One touch from Mike and he would know the entire story thanks to his own unique gift. Mike could pull memories from another's mind. He would see everything that had happened like a video playing just for him. His distinctive abilities helped make him an exceptional detective.

After several minutes, he pulled his hand away. "You were right; he does look like a giant." His lips twitched.

"I told you."

"You forgot to tell me that you clocked Jake. I'm surprised you caught him off guard." The grin on his face and twinkle in his eye meant he approved.

"You and dad taught me well."

"How come you didn't tell me you broke up with Ben?"

It was times like this that his gift was a godsend so she didn't have to try to remember every little detail about her assailant, but every now and then, he was notorious for poking his nose where it didn't belong. She couldn't keep anything from him. The slightest touch of his fingers could reveal more than any brother would want to know.

"He cheated on me. There isn't much left to say." Emma shrugged. She gazed intensely into the fire, trying to make sense of both her lack of emotion from the breakup, and the relief she felt from it being over. Emma had never been in love with him even before the betrayal and should have broken it off sooner.

Mike got up from the couch and started pacing again. Even as a child, pacing was how he had always worked through problems. "Who else is mad at you Em? Do you think he sent the giant after you? Has he threatened you before?"

"No, he was mad and called me a few choice words, but he'd never physically hurt me."

"Exactly what happened?"

"I caught them together in his office. I had a feeling he was hiding something from me, just didn't have any proof. He followed me out to my car, claiming she didn't mean anything to him, and that I had driven him to do it. He insisted it was all my fault."

Emma looked up at her brother. "I didn't buy a word of it, so I left, and the funny thing is, I'm relieved."

Her brother would want to know every detail, but she didn't want to deal with it. Not tonight. Emma sighed. "Can we talk about it tomorrow? I just want to go home and soak in a nice, hot, relaxing bath."

****

Jake let Claire lead him out of the room, aware the siblings wanted to talk. The cryptic messages alone were evident enough. His military training and experience in private investigation and bodyguard work helped him pick up on the subtle clues and body language. Mike and Emma were speaking in some sort of code.

Orchestra music blared as they walked by the ballroom headed for the kitchen. Ladies dressed in black and white ball gowns and men dressed in tuxedos filled the entrance. A combination of strong perfumes hung in the air and threatened to choke him. Jake didn't miss having to attend parties like this.

Once Jake had figured he could make anonymous donations, he'd quit going altogether, unless it was work related. The success of his company, Tactical Maneuvers sometimes depended on him attending all sorts of charity events. He'd opened the personal security business with his old black ops team after his parents died. His team was now the only family he had left.

Even though Mike didn't work for him, Jake still considered him family from their days in the military. Mike had saved his ass more than once and had been there when he found out his parents had died. They'd left him with a huge inheritance these socialites would probably love to get their hands on. His considerable charity donations prior to his anonymity didn't go unnoticed. Countless women chased Jake for the money he had in his bank account. His trust in women diminished when the gold diggers started showing up out of thin air. He wouldn't hesitate to give the shirt off his back to someone in need, and some women tried to take advantage of that. So far, he'd only had unpleasant experiences and hadn't found a woman he could trust; consequently, he had quit looking. His work kept his life chaotic, and he hadn't found a reason to make any changes to his lifestyle yet.

Claire pulled him through the double doors to the kitchen. Wait staff with trays of finger foods and champagne scurried around. He would kill for a beer. No amount of champagne could get him drunk enough at parties like these, and he had tried at several. Jake turned to see Claire staring at him. She hesitated, and Jake was surprised when she bypassed the trays and headed for the fridge. She shoved a bottle of beer in his direction as she reached in for another one.

"How did you know I wanted a beer?"

"You look like a beer drinker to me." Claire continued to stare directly into his eyes, taking in every movement he made. Jake felt like he was under a microscope as he shifted from one foot to the next and rubbed his temple. *Must be jet lag from the trip.*

It wasn't like Virginia was across the world, just a short trip with no layovers. It didn't actually make sense, but that was all he could contribute it to. "Can I get an aspirin?" he asked to break her intense stare and the awkward silence.

"Sure...so you're a friend of Mike's?" she asked as she handed him the two white pills she pulled from the cabinet.

"From the military." He shrugged, not offering her any more detail than was necessary. Jake didn't know how much Mike had revealed to his sisters about that time in his life.

"Are you here on business?"

"Nope, just a vacation...Thought I would drop in on Mike." He took a deep swig of his beer to wash down the pills. The refreshing liquid slid down his throat quenching his thirst. Unfortunately, it didn't do anything to temper the throbbing in his head. Even with all the conversation and clanging of glasses around them, they stood in uncomfortable silence staring at each other again. She was pleasant enough and beautiful too. All the women in this family were stunning. No wonder Mike had kept them a secret. "Well, I guess Mike's going to be a while. I'll show myself out." He threw back his head and drained the beer.

As he turned to leave, Mike and Emma strolled in. "You didn't tell me Emma got a hit on you," Mike accused with pride in his voice.

"Lucky shot." He smiled and winked at Emma.

"Emma gave me the guy's description, and I have to go back to the office and start looking for him. Abby's staying for the party, but can you take Emma home for me? We'll pick up her car tomorrow."

Mike had once trusted Jake with his life, and now that had transferred to his sisters. It was an offer he couldn't turn down. When someone needed his help, he couldn't refuse.

"Of course, I'll make sure she gets home safe. I may even stay in town awhile to help you catch this guy."

Jake motioned toward the door and led her out the same way they'd entered. He made short strides matching hers and placed his hand on her lower back. Butterflies erupted in Emma's stomach. One simple touch made her nervous like a schoolgirl with her first crush.

Emma had had relationships, but they didn't last long. Her relationship with Ben had actually been the longest at three months. Her inability to see his deception had her questioning her abilities. Ben's touch had never given her the tremors she felt from the slightest caress of Jake's hand.

They stepped out to the drive. The night had turned pitch black, and fog had rolled in, leaving a mist covering everything, it touched.

CHAPTER 5

The dampness in the air clung to her hair and clothes, causing a shiver to run down her spine as they made their way to the car. *Maybe the dampness will help.* She chuckled at her thought.

"What's so funny?"

"Just thinking I probably look like a mess. This wasn't how I was planning on spending my Saturday night," she muttered more to herself than to him. "You know, you don't have to take me home. I can call a cab."

"Mike asked *me* to take you home, and I never fail a mission."

"Jake, I'm not your responsibility; besides, I'm sure we lost the guy chasing us." *I hope.*

"Sorry, Emma, you won't change my mind. I told Mike I would see you home, and I intend to." A muscle jerked in his jaw. He seemed set on his actions as he opened the car door for her.

"I'm sorry you have to waste your night on me." Shoulders slumped, she climbed into the car and pulled the door closed.

"Baby girl, this one sure is stubborn." Emma swung around, surprised to see Momma Mae in the backseat, A ghostly chaperone was the last thing she needed tonight.

"Don't I know it," she managed to whisper before he got in on the other side.

"Baby girl, you and your young man need to buckle up." Emma turned and smiled, then she straightened again and tried to cover her actions.

"Nice car," she said as she shifted in her seat, grabbing for her belt and clicking it in place. She noticed he did the same, and she smiled. She considered Momma Mae's request, wondering if it was just a safety issue or a warning of some kind. *Let's hope she just doesn't want us to get a ticket.*

He stopped at the end of the drive and looked at her with a tilt of his lips. "Which way is home?"

"I live at 612 Langford. Take a right and I'll point you the rest of the way."

"No need for directions. I know my way," he said.

"You don't live here. How can you possibly know the way?" *The man that doesn't think he needs direction. Typical.*

"Don't tell me… you have some type of internal GPS?" Sarcasm dripped from her tone. With her own abilities, she couldn't discount the possibility of others with unique gifts.

"Don't be mean to the man, baby girl. He's going to be important to you," Momma Mae warned.

Oh puleeze, this man was just pretty to look at. Several delicious possibilities immediately came to mind. Definitely one-night stand material, but there was no way he would ever mean more to her. Hell, he didn't even live here, did he? She waited for an answer. He just sat there, his gaze wandering over her. What was he thinking? Maybe that she was a nut case? She realized she was being mean to the man her brother trusted, and he was actually doing her a favor. She took a deep breath, inhaling the fragrance of his manly aftershave and exhaled slowly, trying to rein in her inner bitch.

"I'm sorry. I'm not usually this mean."

Jake's smile was unexpected. He sported dimples on both checks. His blue eyes glittered with amusement. When he winked at her, she decided he was definitely one-night stand material. He confused her. One minute she wanted to deck him again, and the next, she wanted to flirt. Emma figured the emotional roller coaster was just from her lack of sleep with Ben calling at all hours and the long, crazy day she'd had. Jake placed his palm on her leg, the heat from his touch warm even through her clothes. He grinned.

"It's okay, Emma, I understand." Making a turn, he continued. "I know where Langford is because I have a vacation house near there. But, no, I don't live here."

Emma nodded. "I appreciate you taking me home. I'm sure you weren't planning on babysitting tonight." Emma offered a sad smile then looked down at her fidgeting hands in her lap.

Jake reached over and took one of her hands in his. Emma couldn't help but notice the hand holding hers. Unfamiliar but strong, his calloused fingers lightly scratched her skin as he caressed her palm with his thumb before he brought it to his lips and placed a gentle kiss. "It's no hardship, Emma. I'm in a town where I only know one person, and I'm with a beautiful woman."

The car came to a smooth stop, and she pulled her gaze from his. She hadn't even noticed they'd arrived. Emma needed to put some distance between them. His proximity was getting to her. She pulled her hand from his and reached for the door handle and gave it a tug. "Thanks for the ride."

She pushed open the heavy door and climbed out, glad to be home at last.

"Wait." Jake insisted as he quickly exited the car. "I need to make sure it's safe."

Emma looked up from digging for her keys in her purse. "That's not necessary. I told you we probably lost the guy." Emma ducked her head and continued digging as she turned to walk toward the door. Jake's hands shot out to steady her when she almost tripped on the sidewalk.

"Emma, don't you ever watch where you're going?" His gentle tone indicated he was just worried, so she didn't snap back.

Emma pulled her keys out and gave them a little shake before she jammed the key into the lock. "Really, I'll be fine."

Jake gently placed his hand over hers, stopping her from turning the key. "Please, Emma, just let me check it out. I'll sleep better tonight knowing that you're safe."

Emma let out a sigh and stepped back, letting Jake take the lead into her house. She followed on his heels, flipping on light switches as she went, scaring off any would-be thieves. "It's really not necessary."

Emma walked to the cherry-wood table in the foyer, opened the drawer, and pulled out her revolver. "I can take care of myself. Mike insisted we know how to protect ourselves."

Jake looked at the gun in her hand, his mouth hanging open, not sure what to make of the little vixen. Remembering the punch she got in on him, he shouldn't really be surprised considering who her brother was. Mike wouldn't leave them defenseless. Jake wondered what other skills she possessed and was dying to find out. "I'm sure you can, Em, just humor me."

Jake continued to walk through her house checking possible hiding spots where a criminal could be lying in wait. He could almost feel her rolling her eyes as he carefully checked the locks on her back door and windows. Jake could learn a lot about a person by their house, but he didn't want Emma any more uncomfortable than she'd already been tonight. He just wanted her safe. Jake followed behind Emma to the door forming a plan in his head, to get to know her better.

Emma pulled the door open and stood patiently with her hand on the knob. He stopped before crossing the threshold. Jake stepped into her personal space, placed his hand on her hip in an intimate touch, and leaned over, gently brushing his lips against hers. He pulled back and watched her eyes slowly flutter open, before walking out the door. Looking over his shoulder, he called out, "Sweet dreams, Emma."

Jake looked back at the brunette, her fingers touching her lips as she watched him walk away. "Don't forget to lock the door."

Jake waited to watch Emma close the door before he put his key in the ignition and gave it a turn. His phone vibrated in his pocket. He knew who was calling; he didn't even need to check the caller id.

"Hey, Mike, I just dropped her off and checked out the place before I left." Jake didn't blame his buddy. If it had been his little sister, he probably would have acted worse. Hell, he probably wouldn't have trusted the guys to keep their hands off of her and would have driven her home himself.

"Thanks, Jake, I knew I could trust you. Listen, I'm going to be busy trying to figure this out, so can you keep an eye on her? I know you're on vacation, and I wouldn't ask if it wasn't important. She needs a bodyguard, someone out of sight that can keep an eye on her and be unseen."

"It's no problem, Mike. I'll watch out for her." Mike didn't have to ask twice. He had saved Jake's ass several times in the military. That was the least he could do for his old friend.

"She'd be pretty pissed at me if she knew that's what I had you doing."

"It's our secret, dude. She won't even have to see me. I'm good at staying invisible. If I notice anything out of the ordinary, I'll give you a call. She's locked up tight for tonight, so I'm heading to the house to get some shuteye, after I make a few trips around the block of course."

Maybe it was safer this way. When he touched her, his mind spun with the things he wanted to do to her little body. His pants tightened at the thought. If he stayed out of sight, he wouldn't be tempted by the little spitfire. Jake didn't think she was like the other girls, hell, she didn't know a thing about his financial status or him in general, and still, he could see the reaction his touch had on her. It was hard to miss the quick intakes of breath and shivers that racked her body. Jake shook his head. Yeah, at a distance would be better. *I'm going to need a cold shower.*

"Thanks, Jake. I'll check in with you tomorrow." Mike disconnected the call. His relaxing vacation had just turned into work, but he wasn't complaining, he would have done it anyway, even if Mike hadn't asked.

When Jake arrived home, he showered and crashed on his bed. The day for him had been exhausting. Not as bad as Emma's, but just a long. It was only minutes after his head fell on the pillow that he'd fallen asleep.

CHAPTER 6

The next morning, Jake groaned when he felt the sun on his face pulling him from his dreams of Emma. The erotic dream had left him hard as a rock. *Damn, another cold shower.*

When Jake emerged from the bathroom, he toweled the remaining water from his hair and shivered. He hated taking cold showers, and it looked like this wouldn't be his last, not if he was watching Emma every day. After dressing, he bypassed the coffee and breakfast, grabbing his keys and heading straight for the café.

He'd expected to find her there, although he couldn't be sure since she didn't have her car. He'd make it a point to make sure she got it back, even if he had to take her there himself, which probably wasn't a bad idea in case the lunatic was still around. Jake had secured a booth in the corner where he was able to see everyone who came and went without having his back exposed. The same waitress from the night before instantly brought him a coffee and a menu then left him in peace. She didn't attempt idle small talk, and he was thankful to be left to his own thoughts. She returned to take his order and promptly left again.

Jake was doctoring up his coffee when Emma walked out from the back. She was beautiful in a girl-next-door kind of way. Her fitted gray slacks emphasized her curves in all the right spots. Her pink sweater showed just enough cleavage his hands itched to hold her ample breast. She was wearing only a hint of makeup today displaying only her natural beauty as she smiled and spoke to the waitress.

Her gaze traveled over the room, taking in the customers, and landed on him. Her smile slipped as she waltzed over to his table and slid into the booth opposite of him.

"Did Mike send you to babysit me, Mr. Donavan?" Emma placed her arms on the table, locking her fingers, and tilted her lips with a smile that didn't quite reach her eyes. She wasn't happy he was here and didn't try to hide it.

"Not at all, Emma. I'm just here for breakfast, but if you need a babysitter, I'm sure I'm up for the challenge. And please, call me Jake." He flashed her a smile that worked on most women, but it didn't seem to be working on her. At least not today. He'd keep his plans to seduce her to himself until Mike found out what was going on. She was a temptation he was finding more difficult to resist.

Emma looked down at her hands and shook her head. "Don't tell me. You're one of those guys."

Jake leaned back and laid his arm over the back of the booth while he studied her. Her tone hadn't been playful; it had been downright accusing, maybe even with a hint of disappointment. It was evident she wasn't falling for his game. "And what kind of guy would that be, Emma?"

"Oh, I'm sure many women have fallen for those dimples and blue eyes and right into your bed with a pick-up line like that." Emma stood and turned her back to him before slowly turning around again. "But, I'm not most women. It was a pleasure to meet you, Mr. Donavan. I do appreciate what you did for me and Abby, but I really must get back to work."

Emma's whole demeanor had changed. She'd done a complete one-eighty on him, and all he'd done was some harmless teasing. *What is going on in that head of hers?* She now held him at arm's length, and he wasn't about to let that slide.

Jake grabbed Emma's hand, momentarily halting her departure. "Emma, you don't know me… but I'd like to change that. I'm not the player you're making me out to be."

Emma lowered her gaze to his face. Searching for something maybe; he wasn't quite sure. He'd been sincere about wanting to know her better. She eased her hand out of his. "I don't think that's such a good idea."

****

Emma's heart sank as she retreated to her office. *It's better this way; he's going to be leaving soon anyway.* Even though that was probably the truth, it didn't make her feel better. The thought of losing her heart when he left wasn't going to be an option; it was better stopping it before it started. Emma stared out the back window and watched the work crews pouring new curb. They'd be done and gone soon, just like Jake. A knock startled Emma, pulling her from her depressing thoughts. She spun around, her lips tilted. Her heartbeat quickened when she thought it might be Jake, but slowed to a steady beat, disappointed to find Claire standing there.

Claire walked in and wrinkled her nose while looking at the new furniture. "I like the old stuff better." Claire pointed back out the door she'd just entered. "Was that Jake leaving?"

Claire bypassed the new furniture and sat in the old brown suede chair, crossing her legs and placing her purse beside her before folding hands in her lap. Emma often wondered where she'd picked up her manners from. None of the rest of her siblings seemed to have them, including her. Emma looked down and frowned. She'd done the right thing pushing him away, but she still could have been his friend. Heck, he didn't know anyone in town. She didn't have to be so rude. Maybe he just wanted to be friends with her. She made a mental note to apologize later.

"He was out there. Did he leave already?"

Claire set her purse by her feet and leaned back into the sturdy chair. Emma felt a prickle in her mind before Claire's assault.

"Stay out of my head, Claire. If you want to know what's going on, all you have to do is ask." Emma smiled at her sister and pulled a mint from her desk, popping it into her mouth.

Momma Mae materialized in the chair next to Claire's. The old ghost didn't speak. She just crossed her arms over her chest and narrowed her eyes.

"Okay, what's going on?" Claire asked while rubbing her arms. "It's freezing in here. Is Momma Mae here?" Claire turned in her seat in a possible attempt to look for the elusive apparition.

Emma rolled her eyes. "She's sitting right next to you and doesn't look very happy."

"Why not? There isn't some axe murderer waiting outside, is there?"

"God, I hope not." Emma's lips tilted, but when she looked over at Momma Mae, she let the smile fall. "There isn't one, is there?" With her luck, she didn't know what to expect anymore and wasn't going to chance it.

"No, baby girl, no axe murderer, but I think you hurt your man's feelings." Momma Mae stood and walked to the window. Emma wondered if she ever missed actually living. If she ever got tired of Emma being the only one able to see her. Momma never talked about her family when Emma asked, but there was always sadness in the ghostly apparition's eyes, sadness that Emma didn't know how to make better for the old woman.

"He's not my man, but I think you're right. He was just trying to be nice, and I walked away." Emma looked at the back of Momma Mae's handmade paisley dress and shook her head in disappointment. She really needed to start thinking of other people's feelings and not just her own. Her mind had been on whether she'd fall for the guy and if it would hurt when he left, instead of seizing the moment and making a new friend, if nothing else. Emma mentally berated herself.

"Who's not your man and what happened?" Claire asked.

Emma explained what had happened with Jake when all she really wanted to do was grab her keys and chase him down to apologize. Her shoulders slumped when she remembered she didn't have her car. The ache in her legs from the three-mile walk this morning should have reminded her.

"I'm sure he'll understand. He seemed like a good guy.

"I'm sure you're right, I'll have to explain the next time I see him. Can you take me to get my car?"

"That's why I'm here, little sister. If you're anything like me, I knew you couldn't live without it for long."

CHAPTER 7

After almost a full week had gone by,
Emma didn't think she was ever going to get
the chance to make amends. She'd thought
for sure Jake would have come into the café
by now and had her staff on the lookout with
specific instructions to tell her. Asking Mike
wasn't an option. He'd turn all big brother
on her and had other things to worry about,
like catching the asshole with the knife.

Heck, even Momma Mae had taken a
hiatus of sorts, leaving her high and dry with
her own thoughts. She'd had plenty to do
now that the work crews had left from
behind her office and she could concentrate

again. Her wandering mind still ended up thinking about him, and her work suffered just the same. By Thursday, she was ready to pull out her hair in frustration. If he didn't come into the café by that night, she'd break down and ask her brother. That was all there was to it.

****

Jake had changed vehicles to an SUV, hoping that Emma wouldn't recognize him because it was a different car with dark-tinted windows. He'd been watching her all week. She'd probably thought she'd run him off, but just the opposite was true. He would just watched her for now, but after Mike caught the guy, all bets were off. Jake would get to know her and see how things went. Something about the little spitfire was drawing him in. He just couldn't put his finger on it. Jake's mouth curved into the beginning of a smile.

Jake shook his head from his thoughts and got back to work, refocusing on his surroundings. Mike had Jake's name added to the guest list for the ball planned for the cancer benefit. Jake needed to be inside to keep an eye on her. He'd had his secretary at Tactical Maneuvers overnight his tuxedo, just for the occasion. Jake glanced down at his watch. Emma would be getting off soon. It had been a long day sitting here, and he would be glad to get out and stretch his legs. She hadn't left the café not once all day.

Movement in his rearview mirror caught his attention. When he turned, there was no one there. Someone had managed to move in on his position, and he hadn't even seen it coming. The little vixen had his mind so preoccupied he'd forgot why he was actually there. Well, enough was enough.

Jake wasn't going to be able to keep her safe from the parking lot. He needed to make sure it had only been his imagination. Jake pulled the gun from the holster, flipped the switch so the interior light wouldn't come on while he slipped from the SUV, and quietly pushed the door closed. Jake ducked and worked his way around the front of the vehicle. That was when he noticed the man lurking in the alleyway. This man looked like a bulky giant. This must be the one who'd been chasing them the weekend before. By the way he studied the building, it was clear his chasing hadn't been random. It didn't take a rocket scientist to realize this guy was up to no good.

The big guy hadn't noticed him yet. Jake inched back around the vehicle and out of his sight, moving in for the takedown. He had parked in the middle of the parking lot so there was an equal amount of distance between him and the psycho and the psycho and Emma's back door. Jake sighed. He was going to have to chase this guy. He wasn't going to be able to take him by surprise. Just when Jake stood, he heard the creak of the heavy door before he saw her.

Emma exited the back of her building and had stopped, her hand on her midsection as she scanned her surroundings. The hulk hesitated. It was apparent he was about to advance on her, but then he paused.

"Jake, what are you doing here?"

Jake's gaze flew from the attacker to hers and back before he pulled his gun and ran for her, blocking her from the giant. There was no way this asshole was going to get to her again. It would be over his dead body.

"What are you doing?" Emma tried to look around him.

"Just stay behind me, Emma. I'm not sure where he went." In the time it took him to reach her, he'd lost sight of the killer. His gaze ran the length of the buildings, but there was no one in sight.

"Who?" Emma asked, touching his arm, bobbing her head around him to see what was going on.

"I'm not sure, but if I had to guess, I'd say it was the same guy that chased you." Jake guided Emma toward the safety of his SUV with a gun in his other hand. His gaze darted left and right for any signs of the asshole.

"Dammit, I did it again." Emma's hands slightly trembled as he got her in and locked her door.

Jake walked the perimeter of the vehicle and got in on the driver's side then started the engine. "You did what again?" Jake asked, never taking his gaze off their surroundings.

"Forgot my gun." Emma was digging in her purse, almost as if it would magically appear.

"I've got you covered." Jake opened the glove box and pulled out a silver revolver like the one she had at home. He checked the safety and handed it to her. Since this guy was a real threat, she was going to have to be prepared. The hate he saw in the hulk's eyes was enough to have him worrying for her safety.

Emma looked from the gun to his face. Her brows pinched together. "Wait a minute. What were you doing here?"

Jake placed his hand on hers. "I was coming to ask if you'd be my date tomorrow night to the benefit, considering I don't know anyone in town."

****

Emma couldn't contain her smile when he mentioned a date. Even with the threat surrounding her, and the guy that was possibly after her, the butterflies in her stomach were for Jake, not the threat. She'd waited almost all week to see him again, and now he was here asking her out, even if it was just because he didn't know anyone else. There was no way she'd say no.

Jake pulled out onto Main Street and headed in the opposite direction from her house.

"I'll go on two conditions." Her voice was barely a whisper.

"Anything, you name it." Jake's dimple returned when he quickly looked at her.

"First, you accept my apology for being so rude to you. I'm not normally like that. Especially considering you're a friend of Mike's. I really am sorry."

Both dimples creased his cheeks. "No apology is necessary, but if that's a condition, then yes, I accept."

Jake turned down another street, two blocks up. He seemed to be canvassing the area, maybe looking for the hulk. "The second, you let me make you dinner so I can make it up to you."

Jake stopped at the red light and looked her way. "Again, unnecessary, but it's a deal. My house or yours?"

"Mine. I've got a confession to make. I've already taken the steaks out and bought some beer. I was going to call Mike to get your number when I got home." Emma could feel the heat travel up into her cheeks. She didn't think she'd have the guts to admit that she'd already planned it, but she'd had no choice. With a psycho on the loose, it was probably a smart idea she wasn't alone tonight anyway. She'd just have to convince her body to keep it simply platonic, and that was going to be a fight. A slight chill filled the car, and Emma glanced back to find Momma Mae in the backseat.

Momma Mae must have been reading her mind, if that was possible. "I've got nothing better to do tonight. Make sure you put in a good movie."

Emma let out a heavy sigh and dropped her head. She may have thought that nothing would happen, but now she totally knew nothing was going to happen. The old bat would run interference. Emma wasn't an exhibitionist.

Momma Mae had stayed true to her word. The meal was delicious and the movie was decent, but the company had been phenomenal. Jake had made her laugh all night. His light touches had set her body on fire while they were snuggled up on the couch, but she'd refrained from jumping his bones. She was getting to know him for the man he was, not for what he did to her body. She was past intrigued and wanted to keep him around. It only made sense that Emma let him sleep on her couch, after all he was a friend of Mike's. At least that was what she was going to tell herself in the morning.

In true gentlemanly fashion, his muscular body was now sprawled on her couch, not where she wanted him to be. Emma felt for the gun under her pillow and fell asleep thinking about her upcoming date with Jake.

CHAPTER 8

Emma blinked awake and inhaled. The aroma of brewing coffee had her on automatic pilot out of her bed and heading toward the smell. She stopped short, and her breath caught at the sight of Jake standing shirtless over her stove. She had felt his muscles several times now but hadn't seen them in the flesh. Now she knew what she was missing. Emma's hand went to her throat. Under her fingers, she could feel the heat traveling to her face.

Her hands itched to feel every dip and curve of his sculpted body. If things went Emma's way, she planned to do just that. She smiled.

"You cook too?" Emma asked while walking to the coffee pot, pouring a cup of the steaming brew.

"I've got a lot more talents than that if you'd care to find out." Jake grabbed the eggs and bacon and put them in the middle of the table.

Emma gripped the counter to keep her hands from taking him up on his offer and exploring his muscular chest. She cleared her throat. "I'm sure you do."

Jake pulled out a chair for Emma and piled a plate of eggs and bacon, way more than she usually ate. Her mind wandered while she ate. He'd protected her, eaten dinner with her, even watched a chick flick, and now he'd done the ultimate and stayed around and cooked her breakfast. The only thing missing was the sex.

Emma craved more than just his light touches and sweet kisses. She wanted to devour this man and see what he could do.

Momma Mae appeared, sitting on the counter and dousing what desire thrummed in her veins. "Baby girl, he's a keeper."

Emma's hand flew to cover her mouth before she spit her coffee all over the table.

"Is it still too hot?" Jake asked as he handed her another napkin.

Emma gulped the remaining liquid and cleared her throat, trying not to look at Momma Mae. Not being able to talk directly to the ghost was sometimes hard to hide.

"Reminds me of my Jonathan. Good looking and sweet too."

Emma wanted so much to ask her more. This was the first time Momma Mae had ever talked about her family, and Emma had so many more questions for the apparition.

Emma wiped her mouth and dabbed her eyes. Momma Mae's comment had been so sincere. "No, not hot, just went down the wrong pipe."

Emma gave a sad smile to Momma Mae. It was obvious she missed him. Her heart ached for the lonely woman. Momma Mae was turned, looking out the window like she was lost in thought.

The rest of the morning was uneventful. Jake hadn't left until Abby showed up. The sisters had a tradition before the benefit. Pedicures, manicures, and the works, all while drinking champagne and telling their favorite stories about their mom. God, they all missed her. It always ended at Claire's house where they continued to get ready. Jake had said he would meet her there and didn't seem too pleased about not being able to pick her up like a real date.

Guests started to arrive right before Jake. Claire had been busy entertaining while Emma hid out in the kitchen drinking a glass of champagne in an attempt to calm her nerves. Tonight she was taking her fate into her own hands. She'd planned her move, running it through her mind all day. She'd purchased lingerie that made her feel beautiful to wear under her black silk dress. Yes, tonight was going to be the night she'd find out all of Jake's other talents.

"Hi, beautiful," Jake whispered in her ear, almost making her spill her champagne. "I'm sorry. I didn't mean to startle you." Jake took her glass and put it on the counter before his strong hands circled her waist and pulled her body to press flush against his.

His hands caressed her lower back, his eyes searching her upturned face before leaning down and placing a chaste kiss on her cheek. The proximity of his body against hers did nothing more than fuel the fire he had started in her body. More determined than ever before, Emma lifted her hands, placing them around Jake's neck and tugged, pulling his lips flush with hers in a sensual dance, determined to have the bone-melting kiss she knew he was capable of. Her hands ran through his brown curls. Jake slanted his mouth, covering hers, and devoured her.

Emma didn't know how she was still standing. His hands caressed her body through the sheer fabric while he tortured her mouth. He tasted like mint, and his hands left a trail of fire everywhere he touched. She could easily get lost in this man. Hell, she'd already had thoughts of skipping the party and finding an empty room.

Someone clearing his throat interrupted her bliss. Jake pulled back and smiled down at her before acknowledging Mike, who stood in the doorway with his arms crossed and a scowl on his face.

"Emma, Claire wants you to meet one of the big sponsors tonight." Mike jerked his head toward the other room in a gesture meant to get her to leave.

Emma looked at Jake, but worry for him had her rooted to the spot. Her brother was downright protective when it came to one of them. Jake nodded in an attempt to tell her it was okay. Emma stopped in front of Mike and jabbed her finger into his hard chest. "I did this, I wanted it, and I'm not done yet, so back off."

Emma turned to wink at Jake before stomping from the room. She'd handle Mike if he screwed this up for her. Emma had almost made it across the mansion when she remembered she'd left her clutch. *Not again.* Her gun and her keys were in there. Emma had sworn to herself to keep it on her at all times until the maniac was caught.

Emma sauntered back toward the kitchen, her mind reliving their shared kiss. Loud voices inside the kitchen had her stopping just outside the door. Mike's familiar tough tone almost drowned out Jake's.

"Mike, I didn't plan it. I was watching her like you asked when the asshole made a move. She found me outside the café, and I was going to ask her to the benefit anyway. I slept at her house to make sure she was safe. Nothing happened."

Angry tears clouded Emma's eyes. He'd only spent time with her because of Mike. He'd led her on, just to be close to her. A lone tear slid down her face. "How could he? I'm so stupid." Emma was left breathless with rage as the humiliation behind it sunk in. She felt the blood rush to her cheeks when she thought of how easily she'd accepted his lie, and the worst part was her brother was in on it. Emma clenched her fist as she stormed into the room and right up to her brother, landing a right hook on his cheek. Mike stumbled back, and Jake lifted a hand to reach for her.

"Don't you dare fucking touch me. Just stay the hell away from me." Emma grabbed her forgotten purse and ran from the room. Her heels clicked on the tile as she ran through the foyer.

Emma ran from the house in a teary haze, her mind racing with everything he'd told her. Even with blurry eyes, she made it to her car and peeled out of the drive, leaving nothing but painful memories behind.

****

Ben stood in the shadows outside the mansion, contemplating his next move when Emma came flying out the door in tears. He couldn't believe his luck. The night was looking up after all. Not only had he been there when Jake had written a two million dollar check for the charity, but he'd also watched Emma leave crying, and without her bodyguard. This night couldn't get any better. Ben pulled out his phone and punched in the numbers.

"If you didn't already see her, she just peeled out of here. She's upset and, more importantly, alone. I need you to take care of this tonight. Do you understand me?" Ben tried to keep his voice low, afraid of being overheard by his colleagues outside smoke their cigars. He'd stay at the party for his alibi, but his worries would soon be over. Oh yes, she was going to pay.

****

Emma glanced again in the rearview mirror and missed her road. Her emotions rolled through her like the lightning flashing through the night's sky. More tears spilled from her eyes as she tried to maneuver the darkened roads. The torrential downpour came on quick, making the roads difficult to see. Horns blared as they passed, barely swerving out of her way. At first, she hadn't noticed the tail behind her, the SUV that was getting closer as she passed every mile marker until he was just about touching her bumper. Emma lifted her hands to her eyes and swiped at the damn tears. She'd known better than to get involved. She'd known better than to trust him. Emma's heart conflicted with her head. Now that Jake was off babysitting duty, he'd be leaving soon. The car following her wasn't even trying to be discreet. The pouring rain made it difficult to see the driver. Emma gripped the steering wheel so hard her knuckles had turned white before she beat it with her palm. "Damn him for not being honest."

The air in the car turned chilly, and Emma didn't need to look to know who'd just appeared. All she wanted to do was be left alone. Momma Mae's soothing voice broke the silence between her sniffles. "Baby girl, you need to go back."

"Like hell I do. He was pretending, don't you get it?"

"Emma, give the man more credit than that. If you had stuck around, you would have seen him stick up to Mike. He's crazy about you. Couldn't you see it in his eyes?"

Emma took her eyes off the road for a brief second and glanced over at the apparition. *Can she be right?*

"Baby girl, I wouldn't lie to you. I might not always be able to tell you what's going to happen, but I won't lie to you."

Emma pondered that, releasing some tension on the gas pedal. She noticed the black SUV swerve like a drunk driver before barely missing her car.

Her head was pounding again, and her stomach churned. *Crap, here we go…Again.*

Momma Mae's voice of reason filled the car. "Baby girl, you need to go back, but first get the hell away from that car."

Emma grabbed her stomach from the pain taking hold. Emma slowed to pull over on the side of the road, and the SUV slowed down behind her. She strained to see through the rain and the SUV's tinted windows but still couldn't make out who the driver was.

"Don't stop, Emma. Get away from that man."

Emma pushed the gas pedal to the floor and clutched the wheel. "This isn't happening again." Emma yanked on her seatbelt to ensure it had clicked in place before she reached down between the seats, grabbed her purse, and pulled out her gun.

"Who the hell is he?" Emma spoke through clenched lips.

The words had no sooner left Emma's mouth than the first impact from the black SUV sent her careening forward. Her head smacked the steering column with a blunt force. *Shit, I'm going to die.*

The seatbelt straining against her body was sure to leave more bruises, though there was no time to worry about that now. The little horses under the hood were kicking into overdrive. Emma's plan was to outrun him. Emma tightened her grip, her palms sweating under the stress. Her knuckles turned white from the intense grip she had on the steering wheel. Emma headed toward Lexington, but she wasn't sure she would make it. The black SUV struck again, this time sending her VW toward the median.

The slick roads made the car hard to control. All she knew was she needed to get the hell out of dodge. Emma glanced in the rearview mirror to see if she was getting away, but there was only black and she heard the noise of another engine, not her own, revving nearby. The driver had turned off his lights, making him nearly impossible to see in the rain, and she only caught glimpses when the lightning flashed. Emma spun the wheel to turn onto Lexington, sending gravel in the air as she hit the shoulder. These highways weren't normally deserted at this time of the night, but it seemed just her luck. She was sure two wheels left the ground at some point. Her heart was beating so fast she thought it would come out of her chest.

Emma said a silent prayer when she hit the potholes littering the pavement, jostling her and making her seatbelt strain. The paving company fixing the bumpy road had left behind their orange barrier cones filled with water stacked along the side of the road. The orange cones practically glowed in the dark, giving her a little relief from the blackness around.

I'm going to die.

"Not yet, baby girl, but it's gonna hurt. Hold on tight," Momma Mae calmly chimed.

"Are you kidding me?" Emma shrieked out of frustration. Her eyebrows creased.

This time the SUV hit hard. Emma's scream filled the car and was drowned out by the back quarter panel crunching under the pressure. The move flipped her car, sending her rolling toward the ditch.

"Oh god!"

"Hang on, Emma," Momma Mae's voice whispered in her ear. "Jake's coming for you."

The reinforced roll bar and her seatbelt held firm as the car rolled toward the shoulder. The smoke in the air from the torn exhaust entered the car through the shattered windows. The rolling would make her sick if the gas fumes didn't do it first. The car skidded, sliding through the rain on the roof into the orange barrels. Water exploded, adding to the rain coming in through the broke window, drenching her, but they had served their purpose. The car skidded to a stop. She hung upside down in her seatbelt, all the blood in her body rushing down to her head, making her thoughts foggy.

Stunned into disbelief, Emma's vision blurred as she tried to keep her eyes open to see if the man was still coming to kill her. The sound of a honking horn and squealing tires passing her told her that he'd taken off. She unbuckled her seatbelt and lowered herself down onto the roof of her overturned car. If she lived through this, it was going to be a miracle. Emma's last thought was that her mind was playing tricks on her, giving her a glimpse of what she desired most. Jake's face was the last thing she saw before her world slowly faded to black.

CHAPTER 9

Emma struggled in the darkness, unable to open her eyes, her mouth too dry to talk and her throat on fire. The familiar beeping of monitors invaded the quiet, and the pungent smell of antiseptic assaulted her nose. The same scent she remembered from her mom's hospital room so many years ago. It gave little relief to know she must be in a hospital. The creaking of a door sounded close by. She thought she recognized the feel of Jake's calloused fingers from the gentle grip on her hand but wouldn't be sure until she heard his deep voice. Frustrated, Emma wanted to scream she was okay, but the words wouldn't leave her lips. She was trapped inside the dark recesses of her mind. The muscles in her throat were dry and protested her actions. Something soft and wet pressed against her palm. *Did he just kiss me?*

His soft voice echoed in her ears. "I'm so sorry, Emma."

Yep, it was Jake holding her hand. Someone needed to oil the damn door because it creaked again. Her brother's demanding voice was unmistakable. "How is she?"

"Still out. They've bandaged her up and run some tests."

The door creaked again as her brother yelled, "Where the hell is the doctor!"

An unfamiliar female voice replied, "Calm down, sir. What seems to be the problem?"

"My sister is lying unconscious in a fucking bed, and you're asking me what the problem is?" She could just imagine his hands flying in the air while he yelled at the poor nurse and paced the room.

"We're waiting on test results, sir." The nurse's voice trembled. "Let me get the doctor for you." The irritating screech of the door filled her ears again.

Another familiar hand took hold of hers. The smooth aftershave Emma had given her brother for Christmas the year before filled the air. She knew his light touch would play the events in his mind. Emma prayed he didn't blame Jake. He was the only reason she was still alive. Mike's hand released hers, and his aftershave dissipated. He'd walked away again and was probably pacing while he sorted out the scenes he had pulled from her.

More determined than she'd ever been before, Emma struggled to open her eyes. She pushed her limits. A sliver of bright light made her squeeze them closed again. A moan escaped her throat. Again, she eased her eyes open and was blinded by the bright white light overhead. She quickly turned her head. Her stomach rolled from the quick movement. Adjusting to the light, Emma slowly turned her head again, relieved her senses hadn't failed her.

Her suspicions were confirmed. She lay in a hospital bed, and Jake and Mike were with her in the room. Emma inventoried her body, lifting the sheets to see the damage. Relief swamped her. Although she'd suffered some substantial bruising, she was thankful all the essential limbs were still attached.

Mike was busy pacing in her small room and hadn't noticed she was awake. Jake noticed immediately. He perched beside her on the bed, leaned over, and planted a chaste kiss on her lips.

"How do you feel?" he whispered. Taking a deep, pained breath, he closed his eyes. "I'm so sorry, Emma."

She placed her hand on his cheek and gave him a sincere smile. "It wasn't your fault," she choked out in a raspy voice. Pain shot through her vocal cords, from her dry throat, but she hid the grimace.

Mike was quickly by her other side and laid a gentle hand on her arm as he kissed the top of her head.

"You scared me."

A prickle ran through her head. Emma raised her eyebrow, unsure if the feelings were leftover from the accident or from Mike poking around. Within seconds, the sensation disappeared. Emma practically salivated when Jake held a glass of water to her lips. She tried desperately to down the contents, but after only a few sips, he pulled it back. The cool liquid relief was a blessing, and she desperately wanted more.

"I'm sorry," she choked out as tears formed in her eyes. Anger, disappointment, and relief swarmed through her thoughts as she tried to force them back. Thankful to be alive, she needed to stay strong for her brother. Emma didn't have to read minds to know Mike would blame himself for her driving while upset. She expected to find Momma Mae had made herself at home in her room, but the old ghost was nowhere to be found.

She turned her head slowly toward Jake. "What happened after I blacked out?" she asked as he once again put the cup back to her lips. She shifted in bed for a more comfortable position and immediately wished she hadn't. Her body ached from the bruises.

"Whoever it was left. I'm not sure if he got spooked when I was blaring my horn or if he thought he had finished the job. I pulled you out of the wreckage and away from the car before it went up in flames. I'm so sorry, Emma." Regret filled his voice.

Emma thought about that for a minute before the word fire registered. "Oh my god! My poor car..."

"Your car can be replaced, Emma. Your life is more important."

"I got your gun and purse out and had a wrecker take it to Abby's lab, maybe the department can give us some clues to help catch this asshole." Mike walked to her side. He grabbed her hand, sitting down on the edge of her bed in silence. His eyes closed, and his eyebrows furrowed together. She knew what he was doing by the concentration on his face. He was pilfering her mind again. Hadn't he seen enough?

Jake opened his phone and called someone. His stern voice was distracting her from Mike's prodding, so she eavesdropped on his conversation.

"I don't care. Edwards, I want you, Jacobs, and Briggs on the next flight. Mike needs our help. I've got the plane on standby." After a few more uh huhs, he flipped the phone closed.

The door flew open again, and Ben and her sisters barged into her now cramped hospital room dressed in tuxedos and ball gowns. *What the hell is he doing here?* She looked at Mike, raised her brow as if questioning who would have invited him to the hospital. All she got was a shrug. Lots of help he was.

"What are you doing here?" Emma asked Ben.

"I was at Claire's party when she got the call from Mike."

He was the last person she wanted to see. "Ben, we're over. You don't need to be here."

The collective gasps from her sisters reminded Emma she'd avoided that conversation with them. She would have a lot of explaining to do later. Emma clenched the sheet, and her jaw ticked. How dare he come in here all concerned like they still had a relationship? What an ass!

Tension filled the room, weighting heavily on her chest as she glared at Ben.

Her gaze flew to her brother again, the only other person in the room who knew the truth. Mike studied her face before turning toward Ben.

"I think you need to leave," Mike said in his big brother tone.

Jake strolled to her and took her hand in his. What was he trying to prove? Why not just give the man more ammunition to stay? Ben was used to getting his way and would now see this as a challenge. Emma's blood boiled. She was going to need to deal with this now once and for all.

Ben glanced from their joined hands to each of their faces. "Sooo, it's like that?" He shook his head in what appeared to be understanding. "Is this asshole why you walked out on me?" he spat out.

"*Get out!*" she screamed, not caring that her throat was still raw.

She closed her eyes, tired of him not taking responsibility for his actions. She didn't want him to assume there was anything left for them to "work out". It was over. Emma released a sigh as she leaned back into her hard pillow, exhausted from the day's events. Clair and Abby walked to the bed, taking a stand by her side as Mike and Jake advanced on Ben.

"The lady asked you to leave." Jake gestured with his hand to the door as he and Mike stalked closer to Ben. The two of them together made an impressive solid wall of muscles.

"This isn't over, Emma." Ben's threat vibrated off the hospital room walls.

"I believe it is, buddy." Jake shoved him toward the door at the same moment it squeaked open. The door slammed into his face, and a loud crack reverberated through the room. Blood drops splattered on his tuxedo shirt as he cupped his hand over his nose.

A petite blonde in a white lab coat stopped inside the door. She must have realized what she had done. Her hand flew to her mouth. "I'm so sorry. Are you all right? Her intent seemed sincere as she approached Ben with an outstretched arm to check his nose. "Damn, I think you broke it. You'll be

sorry for that," he spat out as he hurried
from the room.

Emma was beginning to wonder if she'd
ever truly known Ben at all. His threats
lingered in the air, but she had no headache
other than the dull pain from the accident
and no stomach cramps assaulted her. She
was still safe.

Emma remained quiet. She had little
sympathy for the jerk. Laughter erupted
from Mike and Jake, breaking the silence.
Claire slapped her brother on the arm to get
him to stop. The women's gazes flashed from
the now closed door to the two men creating
a scene. Dr. Lister's hands went to her hips,
and her squinted eyes reminded Emma of her
third grade teacher. Emma smirked, satisfied
her Neanderthals were about to be brought
down a notch by the little doctor. She
expected them to start pounding their chests
at any moment.

"Everyone out," the little doctor
demanded. Emma didn't expect such
command from such a petite thing. Her
authoritative tone commanded respect. *She
must be used to this.* Emma smiled.

"Not a chance, short stuff." Mike pulled
his badge and flashed it. "Who are you and
how is my sister?"

"Dr. Lister, her doctor," she said with a tilt of her head toward Emma. "Now leave so I can do my exam." She made a shooing motion with her hands.

"Doc, all you had to do was ask nicely," Mike said as he approached Dr. Lister. He towered a foot over the petite thing, doing his best to invade her personal space.

Emma watched, impressed as the doc stood her ground and looked up at Mike. With a seductive smile, she winked and replied, "Detective, I run the show around here, and you need to leave so I can do my job." Dr. Lister left Mike standing in the middle of the room, dismissing him, when she turned and walked over to Emma's bed. *Who knew the little doctor could hold her own?*

Her sisters kissed her cheek and left with the threat they would talk later about Ben. They all filed out of the room, but she knew at least two of them weren't going far.

CHAPTER 10

Dr. Lister completed her exam. Emma had a concussion from the accident. It explained her pounding headache since she seemed to be safe. Dr. Lister prescribed medication and gave her the option of being released into someone's care or staying for observation. Either way, she wasn't going to get a solid night's sleep tonight. Emma chose release over incarceration. The quicker she could get out of here, the closer she could come up with a plan to flush her assailant out. Emma was tired of looking over her shoulder and decided to take matters into her own hand. Her brother wasn't going to be happy with her new plan. She just needed to stay out of touching distance until then.

Emma had changed out of her hospital gown and into a pair of scrubs, compliments of Dr. Lister. Emma was hanging up the phone when Mike and Jake walked through the door.

"Who were you talking to?" Mike asked as he walked toward her.

"I had to get someone to cover for me at the café for the next few days," she quipped. "Doctor's orders."

Emma got dizzy as she got off the bed and swayed when the room started to spin. Jake's strong arms came around her for support. She blinked her eyes several times to bring the room back into focus. She hated to rely on anyone but herself.

"Easy, Emma. Do you have a concussion?" Jake asked. She was sure he was still blaming himself for the accident. The last thing she needed was a Greek Adonis posing as her knight in shining armor. Being close to him for any length of time would distract from her new goal, and that wasn't going to be an option. She'd figure out how to keep everyone safe while keeping her secrets held close to her heart. Emma had almost slipped up once, revealing her little secret; she didn't want to risk it again.

"Yeah." She released a sigh. "Someone has to wake me up every hour. I need to go to Claire's or Abby's house for the night." She frowned. Emma didn't want to deal with questions about Ben, but she had no choice. Her sisters would push until they got answers.

"You can't. Claire went back to her party." The cancer benefit was special to all of them. "Abby went to see John, and I need to get back to the office to try and find your thug."

"Well, I'm not staying here. I will just set my alarm clock to wake me every hour."

"Don't be silly, Emma, that won't work." Jake took her arm and pulled it around his shoulders as he clutched her hip, giving her support. Her body ached from the sudden movement, and she grimaced. "You're coming home with me."

"Like hell I am." She tried to pull out of his embrace, but she was too weak. He just held tighter. She tilted her head back to look in his eyes and wondered why this was happening to her. Why did she have to meet a nice guy, albeit stubborn, under these circumstances? The situation obviously called for a different tactic with him. She tried reasoning. "I'm not your problem, Jake. You were just doing a favor for Mike, and as much as I appreciate it, I don't think that's a good idea."

"Emma, first of all, Mike didn't even have to ask. I would have done it regardless." Jake held up two fingers ticking off each of his points. "Second of all, it will give us some time to get to know each other better, and I do believe that you promised not to be mean to me anymore. So under the circumstances, I believe you've just became my house guest...Don't be stubborn, angel, just get used to it." Jake turned his gaze to her brother to discuss plans with him, dismissing her.

"Mike, can you get her car back to her place and bring her some things?

"Yep, I'll be there in an hour."

"Mike, be reasonable," she pleaded. "I can't stay with him. I barely know him."

"I do, and you'll be safe. His place has security like Fort Knox. Em, please trust me."

Even though her brother was a pain in the ass, he was still one of the few people she trusted in the entire world. She would grin and bear it until she could slip away. She needed time to figure out who was trying to kill her before he succeeded. Mike might be the cop in the family; however, Emma was just as resourceful. She had friends on the force and could easily get the information she was after with little more than a few promised dates and batting her eyelashes. Mike had made sure she knew how to defend herself and use a gun. All she had to do was change the playing field. Next time she would be ready for this asshole.

She conceded and smiled at her brother, and without another word, Emma lowered herself into the awaiting wheelchair.

When Jake pulled up to the entrance in the same SUV from before, the SUV reminded her of the one that had run her off the road. Fatigue set in at the thought of trying to climb into the tall monstrosity. Her muscles ached, and her head still throbbed, but fortunately, it still wasn't the type of pain she associated with danger. She just wanted a comfortable bed to lie down in so she could sleep until all of her worries went away.

Emma struggled to get out of the wheelchair. Jake leaned down and swept her up in his arms, holding her close to his body before gently placing her in the passenger seat. He buckled her in and shut the door. She waited for what seemed like an eternity for him to finish talking to Mike. The fatigue too much, she leaned her seat back, snuggled into the leather seat, and prayed the ride to Jake's house was uneventful right before she closed her eyes and fell asleep.

CHAPTER 11

Jake's body covered hers as she lay in his arms. Each kiss drove up her need as she whimpered for more. Her heart beat frantically from his light touch. She should stop him. Jake wasn't from here, and it was only going to break her heart when he was gone. She tried to reason, but her body wasn't listening. His hard body pressed her deliciously into the bed while he kissed a line from her neck to her mouth, devouring her.

All thoughts of stopping him vanished as he dove in kissing her, like she had never in her life been kissed before. His hand rose to cup her neck, slowly inching down to her chest in a gentle caress, leaving a trail of fire in its wake. She ran her fingers through his curly hair and pulled him closer. Her body arched into his touch, silently begging for more. Yes, so much more. That was what she needed.

She heard her name called from a distance. It sounded like Jake, but that seemed impossible. He was still kissing her body. The sound became louder, pulling her from the bliss of Jake's caress. Emma opened her eyes to find the star of her dream sitting beside her on the bed. Damn, it had been just a dream. She felt the warmth creep up into her cheeks and prayed she hadn't moaned aloud.

Emma glanced around the unfamiliar room and wondered how she'd gotten there. His ocean blue eyes fixated on her, the intensity making her squirm. Unable to read his thoughts, she cleared her throat.

Jake shook his head and grabbed a cup from the bedside table. "Sleep well? I'm sorry to interrupt your dream. The smile on your face indicates it must have been a good one."

She took a long sip. The refreshing liquid slid down her parched throat. He waited and watched as she drained the contents and took the cup away, placing it on the nightstand. Jake reached up and pushed a stray lock of hair behind her ear before brushing his fingers down her cheek. The slightest touch sent shivers through her body. She needed to think straight. She couldn't, no, she wouldn't, get attached to this man.

"I slept fine. How long was I out?" She eased into a sitting position.

"About an hour. Are you hungry?" he asked.

Her stomach growled at the mention of food. She placed her hand to her stomach and willed it to stop. "I'm starved, but I'd kill for a bath first."

"I'll start you a bath before I go dig us up something to eat." He rose from the bed and went to the adjoining door. She heard the water running as he came back, an unease evident in his eyes. He stared at her for a moment, then he shook his head, clear with whatever decision he had just made.

"Towels are in the bathroom closet. Help yourself to anything else you need." He retreated out of the room, leaving her alone.

The bathroom was out of a dream. He had started a Jacuzzi-style bathtub. The jets were going to feel like heaven on her bruised muscles. She picked up the bubble bath from the counter and inhaled the flowery aroma. *He must entertain a lot while he's here, unless it's his wife's.* The thought came out of nowhere. She looked into the mirror. Her cheeks were a bright red. *I'm such an idiot, I didn't even think to ask.*

The thought reminded her why she was reluctant to stay with Jake. Emma needed to stay focused on her goal and not on Jake, because her goal did not include him. Still, she gushed at the measures he'd gone to in order to make her comfortable. A virtual stranger she hadn't even known existed several weeks ago had taken her in. Of course, it had all been as a favor to her brother, she reminded herself. It was still noble, and she knew Ben wouldn't have done so much as lift a finger without complaining.

Emma eased her battered body into the awaiting bath. The warmth invaded her bones as the jets caressed her skin, making her body feel boneless. The stress from the day had drained her mind, body, and soul. After washing her hair, she leaned back and closed her eyes. She'd sleep like the dead when she lay back down, even in an unknown house.

"How do you feel, baby girl?"

Momma Mae's unexpected voice startled Emma from her relaxation. Was there no place off limits to those in the afterlife?

"Like I got hit by a truck."

"Emma, are you okay in there?" Jake asked from behind the closed door.

"Crap," she whispered to herself. She raised her voice. "I'm fine. I'll be out in a few minutes." When she heard the bedroom door close, she let out her breath.

"He's going to think I'm mental if I keep talking to myself," she whispered to Momma Mae. She had never slipped up revealing her abilities so many times in her life. Something about Jake made her feel at ease, comfortable in a way she'd never felt.

"You need to tell him."

"Oh no I don't! He won't believe me. He'll probably try to have me committed."

"Give him a chance, Emma."

"I can't, Momma Mae. I don't trust him yet."

Emma leaned back and closed her eyes once again. When she reopened them again minutes later, Momma Mae had vanished. The stubborn old woman would be back in

full force later, pushing and prodding until
she got what she wanted. She always did.

Emma wrapped a fluffy white towel
around her as she climed out of the tub. She
grabbed a brush from the countertop and ran
it through her tangled hair then slathered
some lotion along her skin, skipping all of
her cuts and bruises she inspected along the
way. She saw some much needed pain
medications in her future.

Emma grimaced looking at the scrubs
laying on the floor. She longed for her own
clothes, something softer against her skin,
something to wear that was hers. She needed
something to wear. Jake had already been
out in the room once while she was in the
tub, so she wasn't taking any chances. She
slowly opened the door and peeked out,
scanning the room, ensuring she was alone
before emerging nervous and wrapped in a
towel.

Emma was getting ready to rummage
through his drawers and closet for clean
clothes but stopped short when she noticed
her pink suitcase sitting on the bed. She
looked up to the heavens and whispered her
thanks. She smiled, happy to have her own
things until she saw the contents inside. Her
new, comfortable pajamas weren't packed.
Oh no, leave it to her brother to pack her old,

ratty pair instead of the pretty ones. Jake should have asked one of her sisters to do her packing.

After dressing, Emma opened the door and became lost as she explored the house, so she followed the faint voices she heard. Curiosity tempted her to peek in one of the four doors on her hall. *How many rooms does this place have?* There were no pictures hanging on the wall that would give her a hint to the occupants. She reached for the door handle to the room next to hers and stilled, hearing the voices in the distance growing louder.

"She's in the shower." That voice was familiar: Jake's.

"I can't believe he never told us about them," an unfamiliar voice responded.

Oh god, what did they find out and by who? Emma chewed her bottom lip as she inched closer to the end of the hall, not at all sure what she'd find. She rubbed the dampness off her hands on her pajamas as she peeked around the corner. *I could never be a spy.* She wasn't the sneaky type. She straightened from her crouch and cleared her throat as she rounded the corner to stop on a landing. The grand staircase descended on both sides down into a big foyer. Jake stood below with a large blond man. He was just as tall as Jake with his arms crossed on his chest. Dressed in fatigues and a black shirt that stretched over his chiseled muscles, he looked like he'd just come from a mission. *Now, he could pass for a spy.* She chuckled.

"Why did you call us here?" the blonde man asked.

Emma descended the stairs and stopped in front of them. Inhaling a deep breath, she cleared her throat. "I'd like to know that too." Hands on her hip, she tapped her foot and waited for a response. It wasn't her business, but she had a nagging suspicion she was the topic up for discussion.

The blond man looked from Emma to Jake. "Now I know why," he said with a sly grin as he slid closer to Emma.

"Back off, Edwards," Jake sneered. "Emma, this is Butch Edwards." Jake took her elbow and guided her down the hall and toward the swinging double doors. He didn't turn once to see if Butch followed, but she glanced back and was rewarded with a wink. The doors pushed open. Emma stopped, and her jaw dropped as she took in the enormous kitchen. She wondered what it would be like to have a kitchen this size. And this clean. It was bigger than she had at the café.

It sparkled and smelled lemony fresh. The granite counters and tile floor were

immaculate. Emma wondered if he really
lived here at all. No stray dishes or glasses
littered the counter, and there were none in
the sink. No pizza boxes or beer cans either.
This wasn't the typical bachelor pad she'd
expected. She walked around the room,
trailing her finger over the counters,
admiring all the space. Emma stood next to
the island, tilted her head back, and looked
up. Hanging above the island were brand-
new stainless steel pots and pans, high
enough only a giant could reach. She balled
her fist by her sides. Her hands twitched to
grab one and start cooking. She might need a
ladder to get them down, but she would find
a way.

Emma walked to the French doors and
strained to see through the darkness. All she
could make out was the enormous deck. She
turned from her new spot and glanced once
more around the room. There were no frills
or personal items on the counters, and the
walls were empty. Maybe that was the way
he liked it; either him or his wife. She
shrugged. A dog bark broke the silence,
making her jump. She was a nervous wreck.
Her heart raced as she spun too quickly back
towards the door. Blood drained from her
face as the dizziness assaulted her. She

grabbed the closest countertop to gain her balance and closed her eyes.

Butch walked to the doors, pushed them open, and yelled, "Hush, Maxine!" He turned back to her. "I'm sorry, Emma, it's just my dog. She's really a big baby."

"Don't overdo it, Emma," Jake warned. He placed an arm under her legs and one against her back and scooped her up in his arms. His steel arms encased her and pulled her close, causing her to wince. Her tender body still ached from the accident. Emma fought the urge to rest her head on his shoulder as he strolled toward the chair and eased her down. Her stomach growled and broke the uncomfortable silence. Propping her elbows on the table, she hid her face in her hands; sure her cheeks were red from embarrassment.

Jake and Butch chuckled. "Is an omelet okay?" Jake asked as he started to pull ingredients from the fridge.

"Sounds good to me." Butch plopped down next to her, leaned the chair back on two legs, and locked his fingers behind his head.

Emma couldn't take her eyes off the man who sat inches away. He seemed comfortable in any situation, at ease even her presence. This must be nothing new for him.

He was quite the looker; his relaxed persona contradicted his chiseled face and tattooed arms. A chance meeting with Butch in an abandoned alley would have scared the shit out of her. He wasn't going anywhere, anytime soon, and she wasn't asking him to. As she pulled her gaze from his body up to his eyes, Butch had a goofy grin on his face, and he winked. Heat traveled to her cheeks as she looked away.

"Jake, I'm sorry Mike dumped me on you. I'll be out of your hair in the morning." Emma's shoulders slumped as she stared down at her hands, unable to look him in the eyes. She didn't want to be a burden on anyone.

"He didn't, Emma. I insisted, remember?"

"You going to fill me in now?" Butch asked from his comfortable position. Emma started fidgeting with her hands.

"Someone's after her, and I need help protecting her until I find out what's going on and deal with it."

Emma's head shot up. "Now wait just a minute! Who appointed you my keeper?"

"I did."

"Only for the night. I won't put you in danger too."

"What do you mean *too*?"

"I'll fill you in later, Butch," Jake sighed.

Jake had his hands on the counter with his head down. He drew in a deep breath then released it slowly as though making a decision before lifting his head to look up at her. He seemed to have made up his mind. "Em, did Mike tell you about me?" He gestured with his hand toward Butch "About us?"

She looked from Jake to Butch, and her eyes widened. It made perfect sense. She wanted to kick herself for not noticing it sooner. She thumped her hand against her forehead. "Oh I get it! You're gay," she said in a singsong voice as she pointed back and forth between the two of them.

"The hell I am!"

"It's okay, honest." Her hands went up in surrender. "I work with a gay guy."

The chair landed with a thump as Butch sat forward again. "Have you lost your mind? Do we look gay?"

"Well…" She paused and looked both of them up and down. "You're both hunks. So I thought either gay or married." She shrugged and felt her lips raise to a grin.

"Neither gay or married," Jake said as he turned back to whisking the eggs. "We were in the military with your brother. He didn't talk about us?" He glanced her way with his eyebrows raised.

"Nothing specific. He tried to keep us from worrying."

"We're in security, Emma, and I've just made you our next assignment."

Kate Allenton

CHAPTER 12

Emma ate in silence, and the men were quiet, allowing her time to think. Her mind raced as she tried to figure out what to do. The aroma of her cheese omelet, normally a favorite of hers, made her stomach churn. The internal questions weren't the only things making it impossible to enjoy her meal. She sat picking out the veggies she wasn't about to eat.

He could potentially be an asset if what he said was true. He might be able to help her set up the trap and flush the lunatic out. He'd already proven he had skills. Could she risk falling any harder for Jake, a man she knew next to nothing about? The choice could save her life or break her heart. Hiding her secret would be a struggle, but she'd managed before. Her previous near slip-ups had happened under duress. At least she kept telling herself that as justification.

The decision made in her mind, she pulled her shoulders back, looked him in the eyes, and cleared her throat even though accepting help made her feel insignificant and not in charge of her own destiny. *Well, I'll be damned. Didn't Momma Mae mention destiny twice since meeting Jake? That stubborn apparition knows more than what she says.* Emma liked being able to handle things for herself, but she wasn't stupid. She needed all the help she could get. Fighting the butterflies in her stomach, all she managed to choke out was "Thank you, I could use your help."

Jake let out a breath, and his lips quirked as he looked from her to Butch. "I told you she was beautiful and smart," he said as he winked in her direction. "Emma, you look exhausted. Why don't you go get some rest and I'll check on you in a bit."

"I am tired." Relieved she wasn't alone and would have help, she stood up and said "good night" on her way to the door. She turned to her savior one last time. "Thank you for rescuing me tonight. I wouldn't be standing here if it weren't for you."

"You're welcome, Emma."

*****

For the next few hours, Jake and Butch discussed how they would handle Emma's threat. He knew the sisters wouldn't like the plan they came up with, but he'd convince them it was in their best interests. For the second time that night, Jake went upstairs to check on Emma and wake her up. She mumbled in her sleep, carrying on conversations with whomever occupied her dreams. As he walked to the side of her bed, she screamed. Her head thrashed back and forth as though she was fighting an invisible ghost from her dreams.

When she screamed "no!" and tears streamed down her temples and into her hair, he sat next to her and shook her awake, trying to drag her away from the monsters chasing her.

She sat up swinging, not fully awake from her nightmare. Her glazed, teary eyes fixed on him. Her face started to release from the scrunch when recognition hit her. She latched onto his neck in a tight grip and pulled him close. He didn't budge. His heart beat faster as he took several deep breaths. All his muscles flexed as he thought about the attacks on her from earlier. He couldn't wait to strangle the bastard she feared in her sleep. Emma sobbed into his shirt; tears soaked into the cotton making the material damp against his skin.

He rubbed her back in slow circles as he whispered in her ear. "It's okay, Emma; it was just a dream."

"They were dead...my sisters were dead. It seemed so real. The asshole had killed them. I thought I'd lost them." She hiccupped as she tried to compose herself.

"Everyone's safe, baby; it's okay," he assured her as he continued with the slow circles.

She slowly released his neck, wiped her tear-stained face, and laid her head back down. He wouldn't let the psycho hurt her or her family.

"Get some more rest Emma. Everything is going to be okay." Jake rose from the bed, heading toward the door.

"Jake," she whispered. Her voice cracked.

He turned around with his hand on the door. "Yeah, baby?"

"Promise me… you won't let him touch my family. They come first… Promise me," she pleaded.

"We'll protect them, Emma. You have my word."

She let out a breath, closed her eyes, and he watched as exhaustion pulled her back into a now peaceful sleep.

****

Jake told Butch the promise he'd made as he walked him out the door. Butch was going to meet the rest of the team and fill them in with their new assignments.

"The threats are against Emma, right, not her family?" Butch asked, his arms crossed and brows furrowed.

"She's right, Butch, think about it. She's tight with her sisters. If this asshole is smart, he'll use them as leverage to get to her. We need to keep them out of the equation."

They were going to need Emma's help convincing her sisters the danger was as much of a threat to them as it was to her. If they were anything like Emma, the men were in for a hell of a fight. They planned to meet up in the morning to go over the situation. Jake locked the door behind Butch and dragged himself to his office. The day's events had taken their toll on his body. On one of the nine monitors that hung on the wall, he watched as Butch loaded Maxine in the truck and headed down the drive. He flicked the perimeter switch active when Butch cleared the gate then turned on the rest of the house security so he could call it a night, well, actually the morning.

He glanced at the clock, and the red numbers read two in the morning. He needed a shower to ease the tensions in his shoulders. Satisfied the perimeter was secured, he staggered to his room. Even after only knowing Emma a few weeks, his heart had almost stopped beating when he saw her car and battered body inside. She'd come to mean a lot to him in such a short time, he refused to let anything else happen to her. He wouldn't risk losing her again.

After his shower, Jake lay in bed, exhausted, unable to fall asleep. Thoughts of Emma's bruised body plagued his mind every time he closed his eyes. *Damn it! I should have been more careful. She almost died because of me. Maybe she would be safer with Butch.*

The way Emma had saved her sister with her quick thinking and determination impressed him. She was strong, smart, and beautiful and was willing to face her demons head on.

No other person from his past had ever been so fearless and determined fighting the things that scared her most. *Except Jane.* He let out a pent-up sigh and tried to push the thought from his head. He would have killed any man that threatened his baby sister. His heart ached as memories flooded back. If he had paid attention to the ten-year-old pipsqueak like his parents had told him to, he would have had time to save her from her icy death.

He'd been trying to impress a girl, a girl whose name he couldn't even remember. Jane had wandered off toward the dock a few yards away, determined to overcome her fear of the water and swim with him the next summer. She'd fallen into the lake. Fear had squeezed his heart, and he'd run as fast as his feet would carry him, trying to reach her in time, but the freezing water played havoc with her body temperature.

Despite his best efforts, he hadn't made it to her in time before she'd taken her last breath and inhaled the deadly water. Death took her because he had failed to save her. Later he learned the reports indicated she had slipped and hit her head before tumbling into the icy cold lake water. He didn't know at the time she was unconscious. In the next week, he had stood over her grave. Through tears and grief at the age of sixteen, he whispered a vow to her—no matter what the cost, he would grow up to be a man she would have been proud of. A better man than the miserable brother he'd turned out to be.

She had been as fearless and determined as Emma. They each had a heart of gold and believed in him. Had Jane lived, he thought she'd be just like Emma, stubborn and beautiful, but he would never know. His grief got easier as the years passed, but she would always hold a special place in his heart. He pushed those thoughts out of his head. Staying focused was vital if he was going to be half the man he had vowed to be twenty years before.

Emma's vulnerability made her that much more real. Jake knew she had swallowed her pride to accept his help, and he wouldn't let her down. He would keep her safe; he was compelled to keep her safe.

Twice now on his watch, she'd almost died and that was unacceptable. *Just like Jane.* Keeping a clear head would be difficult. All he had to do was get an eyeful of her curvy body, and he was ready to go caveman and throw her over his shoulder and carry her off to bed. When this was over, that was just what he planned on doing.

Jake grabbed his bed linens and found himself headed to the door. Destination set, he walked two doors down and lightly knocked. He put his ear to the door and strained for any hint of sound, but no answer or noise from the other side would stop him from going in. He walked to the bed. Her sleep was quiet, and her breathing was steady. No more tossing and turning from the previous dream. It was the first good rest she'd had tonight. He kissed her forehead and rearranged the chairs next to the bed. He sat in one and propped his legs in the other. Jake settled in for the night, close enough to watch over her but far enough away to give her space.

He checked the alarms on his watch to make sure everything was set. The vibration and beeping would wake him in case of intruders. Proud of his own invention, he smiled. Emma's room didn't have the security setup like his room and office, so for now, the monitoring would be limited to the device on his wrist until he could have it changed.

He had never felt so protective of a woman before was his last thought as he drifted off to sleep.

CHAPTER 13

Waking from her sleep, Emma blinked against the sun streaming through the window, the rays warm on her face. She stretched her sore arms above her head and arched her back when memories of the day before came crashing back. Her hand flew to cover her gaping mouth when images of grabbing Jake and, worse, crying on his shoulder appeared in her mind. She cringed and groaned, closing her eyes, wishing the images would disappear. *He must think I'm a big baby.*

She slowly sat up, getting a better look at the room. At the foot of the bed, two chairs faced each other. A pillow and a folded blanket sat neatly placed in the chair. *Jake.* She smiled. Every tiny considerate gesture he showed managed to tear down another brick she had placed around her heart. A tear slid down her face, and she groaned once more as she swiped at the unwelcome tear. *God, I'm so freaking emotional... I must have PMS.*

Before she finished her thought, Jake was standing in the doorway, his muscular body perched against the frame. "Do you need me to hold you again, baby? I don't mind." A grin teased on his lips.

"Must you insist on calling me that?"

"Yes, but don't worry, Emma; it will grow on you."

He was teasing her, possibly to break the awkwardness from her mental breakdown she'd had last night. With cheeks on fire, she conjured up a smile and in a sweet southern accent replied, "I'm not so sure, honey bear."

She winked as she rose from the bed and headed for the bathroom. With her hand on the knob, she let her smile slip, turned, and with a more somber voice, said, "Thanks."

"Aw shucks, baby. It was all my pleasure."

He straightened to his full height, and his eyes twinkled as he approached her. His tall frame hovered over her five-foot-six body. Her body wanted to lean into him. She forced herself to keep her ground. He leaned down and pressed his soft lips against hers as he pulled her into his embrace and tight against his body. Had she died and gone to heaven? After her pitiful display the night before, crying like a child still scared of monsters, he still wanted to kiss her? As he pulled away, she noticed the dimples she had come to love on his cheeks. He smiled.

"Good Morning, Em." He leaned over and planted another quick kiss on her cheek. "Breakfast is in fifteen minutes. Don't be late or there won't be any left." He smacked her on the butt and headed out the door.

He must not have a lot of food in the house if it's going to be all gone before I get down there... She hurried through the process of getting cleaned and emerged dressed twenty minutes later. Her stomach grumbled as she opened the bedroom door.

She bounded down the stairs with a bounce in her step, fresh from getting some sleep and her shower, toward the sound of male voices coming from the kitchen. She stopped at the doors, drew in a deep breath, and pushed through to greet the unexpected company.

Her brother rushed to her, grabbed her up in a bear hug, and twirled her. "Mike, put me down!"

"Awe, Em, what did you expect? I almost lost you last night."

"Hurting more of my ribs isn't helping." She screeched as he continued to squeeze.

Mike placed her feet on the floor and held on to her for a minute, getting his own personal updates since he'd left her at the hospital. He must have been satisfied with the outcome. He sat back down and started in on the plate full of food in front of him.

"You weren't down in fifteen minutes, Emma, but I managed to save you a plate before these pigs ate everything."

Mike and Butch were the only familiar faces at the table. She smiled at the newcomers as Jake walked to her, leaned down, and planted another soft kiss on her lips.

"I suggest you take your hands off my baby sister," Mike said, interrupting their kiss.

Emma rolled her eyes. "I'll deal with you later."

She grabbed Jake by the collar of his shirt and pulled him toward the French doors out on the deck. "You! Come with me now!"

Outside, and out of earshot, Emma turned to Jake. "Why did you do that?"

"Isn't it obvious?"

"Jake, be serious. Not that I didn't like it, but why would you do that in front of Mike?"

"I wanted the other guys to know you're off limits."

"Why?"

"I don't want the other guys to lose focus. If they think you're with me, then I don't have to worry about it. They'd never make a move on my girl."

Emma was sure in his warped male mind he thought he was helping her cause. "Okay, let's say I buy your excuse. How are we going to play this?"

"That's the easy part. We act like a couple. Everywhere you go, I go, until Mike and I figure this out."

Pretending to be a couple was a potential for disaster. She wasn't sure her heart could handle the games, but really, what options did she have? He was right, and she knew it.

"Okay, but you get to tell Mike." She smiled, walking back inside, and left him standing on the deck with a stunned expression. Well, it was his idea, so he got the pleasure of dealing with her overprotective older brother. She smirked as she made her coffee then sat down in one of the few empty chairs at the table.

Mike's gaze caught hers when she took her first sip of the breakfast morning blend. The steaming liquid felt like paradise on her parched throat.

Mike planted his arms across his chest, his left eyebrow raised. "Did you forget to tell me something?"

"Nope, but Jake did."

He got up from the table, sent his chair screeching backwards, and headed outside where Jake waited.

The yelling that came from outside couldn't stop her smile. She glanced at the newcomers and introduced herself.

Butch slid his chair closer to her. "Where are my manners? Emma, this is Jacobs, and this is Briggs; they're a part of our team."

Jacobs stood and rounded the table. She craned her neck to look at him as his six-foot frame towered over her. He stood out from this bunch; he was dressed in a black suit that looked tailored to fit his scrumptious body. He took her hand and kissed her knuckles. Heat rushed up her cheeks. Emma could tell this one was a heartbreaker. Jacobs was handsome. His green eyes glinted from the sun shining in the window. She bet his smile made a lot of woman weak in the knees and he left broken hearts wherever he went. "It's a pleasure to meet you, Emma."

"Oh, the pleasure is mine," she rasped out, and fanned her face.

All of these men were eye candy, but they didn't hold a candle to Jake. He made her heart skip a beat and sent her hormones into a frenzy.

Butch put his arm around her shoulders and glared at the tall man. "She's off limits."

"I'll let the lady be the judge of that."

Jake and Mike, no worse for wear, walked back inside at that exact moment. Each approached Jacobs from behind with their arms crossed and glared at Emma.

"Sorry, Jacobs, but he's right. I'm apparently off limits."

"Sweetheart, we can change that."

"Weeks ago, I might have agreed, but he's right. I've fallen for Jake." She placed her hand over her heart. "He's stolen my heart." She grabbed his hand and squeezed. Unsure if she'd passed the test, he kissed her knuckles again, nodded, and returned to his seat. The tension in the air seemed to fade when they all sat back down, started eating, and made small talk. The reason they were all there hung in the air unsaid, making her uncomfortable.

Briggs didn't appear to be a man of many words. Emma tried to break the ice by starting a conversation, but a few grunts were her only reward. Emma noticed when Briggs stood to take his dishes to the sink that he was the tallest of all of them. He easily stood six-foot-six dressed in fatigues and a brown shirt that stretched over his bulging muscles. He was another looker. A slight scar marred his face at the temple, and a black tattoo poked out from under his shirtsleeve. Emma thanked god he was on her side.

After sizing everyone up, she waited for Briggs to sit down. She looked at Mike and Jake. "So what's the plan?"

Jake glanced at Mike, who nodded as if giving his approval to proceed, and turned to smile at her.

"I already told Edwards, Jacobs, and Briggs what has been going on. I just haven't told them my plan."

"And what might that be?" Emma asked.

"Well, angel, you're with me. Butch, I want you to guard her baby sister, Abby. Briggs, you get detail on Claire, and Jacobs, I want you to shadow Emma's nephew, John. The threat seems to be directed at Emma, but until we find out more, we can't chance that this guy wouldn't use her sisters to get to her."

"They aren't going to like your plan, big guy."

"That's where you come in, Emma. You get to help me convince them."

"I'll do anything to keep my family safe," she said as she eyed the men sitting at the table. "Gentleman, I'm sure you're very skilled but don't underestimate my sisters. They're resourceful and stubborn."

Butch slid closer to her and put his arm around her shoulders again. "Now, sweetheart," he said with a smile. "You're challenging our manhood. We can keep a few little lassies safe."

"Butch, my sisters will take your manhood, chew you up, and spit you out. I'm trying to give you fair warning. When they feel threatened, or anyone in our family is threatened for that matter, all bets are off. They won't see you as protectors. They'll see you as someone standing in the way of them being able to keep me safe. I'm telling you this to help you. I *need* you to keep them safe."

"I'll consider myself warned, sweetheart." He strode to the coffee pot for another cup.

Determined, Emma marched over and invaded Butch's personal space. She poked her finger in his chest. "Listen here, you ass. If you let anything, and I mean anything at all, happen to one of my sisters, there won't be a place on earth you can hide from me. I'll track you down myself."

He grabbed her hand to stop the poking motion. "What are you going to do to me when you find me, *sweetheart?*"

Jake and Mike flew out of their chairs. Mike held Jake back because Mike knew what she was capable of. Hell, he'd taught her.

In a move so quick Butch didn't see it coming, Emma spun out of his grip and bent at her knees. She swung around with her leg extending, sweeping his feet out from under him and dropping Butch on his ass, just like she'd done on the bald giant.

She leaned down to get in his face. "Don't make the mistake of thinking you know me. You don't know anything about me or what I'm capable of. If you're as good as Jake and Mike think you are, you need to bring your A game when you deal with either of my sisters." She straightened to her full height, took Butch's freshly made coffee off the counter, and walked back to the table.

Momma Mae materialized and was seated in her chair. "Baby girl, be sweet to these men. They are just trying to help you."

Sometimes it was downright annoying she couldn't just talk or argue with Momma Mae when others were around.

Jake put his arm around her shoulders and kissed her forehead. He whispered in her ear, and his breath sent a shiver down her spine. "What other secrets are you hiding from me?"

"Baby girl, you need to tell him."

Momma Mae's statement and Jake's question made her still. Her muscles tensed under his touch. She looked at her brother with her brows raised and tilted her head sideways in a plea for help.

"Jake, she's *my* sister. Honestly, what did you expect? They had to learn to protect themselves when I wasn't around. I taught her more than that little move." Mike beamed at his best friend.

Butch pushed his muscular body up from the floor and approached her. Jake's arm tightened around her shoulders before he pulled his arms away and made to step in front of her, but Butch held up his hands in surrender. He stepped closer, taking her hand in his.

"I'm sorry, Emma. I underestimated you, and I promise I won't do the same with either of your sisters. You have my word." He smiled, raised her hands to his lips, and pressed a quick kiss before looking at Jake with a grin.

Some woman somewhere must have taught all of them that kissing a woman's knuckles was a sign of respect. Her brother must have missed that etiquette class. She had never seen him do such a thing.

"I would say I'm sorry, but I'm not. I need you to understand what you're up against, and that's just from my sisters, not to mention this maniac set on killing me."

"You did. Oh, and by the way, if you ever come to your senses and dump Jake, I'm available." Butch winked and sat back down.

Heat flooded her cheeks as she stared in disbelief. She cleared her throat. "Um, I... uh, I'll keep that in mind."

CHAPTER 14

Emma dumped her coffee in the sink and rinsed her cup, looking out the kitchen window in front of her. The sun was shining. It was going to be a glorious autumn day, too beautiful to be stuck inside all day. She wanted to get out and forget about the events from the day before, but there was still too much to do. Jake came up behind her, placed his hands on the counter, trapping her where she stood, and whispered in her ear.

"It's going to be okay."

Her gaze and shoulders dropped, and she let out a sigh, leaning into his body to savor the feel, if only just for a moment. "I hope you're right. I need to talk to my sisters." She pushed back into his body to navigate some space and moved out of his embrace.

"Mike, I need you to break the news to Claire and Abby and find out where John is. You get the honor of introducing them to their babysitters. So far, this maniac only knows that Abby was with me on the run since the only other person he saw was Jake. I need to keep my distance until we find this guy. The fewer targets he has the better. If they give you fits… *when* they give you fits about having babysitters, have them call me, and I'll handle it."

"Over the phone?"

"Yep, I'll handle it. Jake, grab your keys; you're driving."

"Where are we going?"

"I need to check in at the café, and I need more stuff from my house."

"Give me ten minutes." He strode from the room.

He left Emma standing there with a table full of men staring at her. "I'm sorry for getting you guys involved. Thanks for helping me."

Her heart felt heavy as she left to gather her things. When she opened the door to her room after grabbing her purse, she ran into a familiar brick body. Jake crowded her in the wide hallway, and the warmth of his smile was infectious. Emma balled her fist to keep from reaching for his handsome face and stroking it, but his pull on her heart was something she would need to deal with later. The more time she spent with Jake, the harder it became imagining her life without him.

He placed his palm on her face. "Ready to go, angel?"

His light touch sent shivers through her. His eyes searched for something in hers. "As ready as I'll ever be."

He gently grabbed her hand and placed it in his. "Don't forget we're joined at the hip. Kissing and public displays of affection are a must." He steered her toward the door. "I'll be able to keep you safe if you stay close to me."

Having Jake glued at the hip for too long was a recipe for disaster. Emma needed to solve this riddle quick and get back to life as she knew it. Jake had the means to crush her without even knowing it, and she couldn't give him the chance.

The wind ruined her perfect hair day. The unruly mass was whipping in her face as she made her way to the SUV. Emma added ponytail holders to her mental list of necessities. Today she would regroup, get her bearings, and create some sort of plan that didn't include her death. Her sisters would meet their new guards, and she needed to help convince the she-devils to accept what help they were offering.

"Follow Lexington and take a left on Main. We need to go to the café first. I need to introduce you around so people will buy that we're a couple."

"What should I know about you to make this believable, Emma?"

"There isn't much to tell. You've met my family, well, all of them but John anyway. My nephew is eighteen, just graduated high school, and I think he's off with some friends during a school break before he starts college. You know where my business is, and you've met my ex. I would say you know more about me than I know about you. So tell me, Jake, what makes you tick?"

"That's a loaded question." He glanced at her, and the twinkle in his eye made his response even that much more accurate.

"Tell me something about yourself. Where is your family? Do you have any brothers or sisters? Where did you grow up? Where do you live now? Is there an ex-wife or girlfriend in the picture? Take your pick." If she kept digging into his background, she hoped he would lay off hers. The risk of exposing one of her secrets was too great.

After several moments, he grabbed her hand and kissed the inside of her wrist. "There's no ex-wife, and the ex-girlfriend is ancient history. The guys are my family now because my parents died when I was in the military, and my baby sister died when I was a teen."

"Oh god, I'm sorry." Emma looked from his somber face to her hands clasped in her lap. She knew what it was like to lose a loved one, and he'd lost his entire family.

"It was a long time ago. I grew up in North Carolina, but the last time I visited your brother, I liked it enough to buy a house here. I currently live in Virginia, where my business is located. When I need a vacation, I come and visit. I'm actually surprised I haven't met you before now."

He pulled up in front of the café, and she grimaced. The rumor mill was going to get a fair bit of gossip. He got out and walked around the SUV, scanning the area as he opened her door. Hesitant at first, she met his smile and took the hand he offered. Jake pulled her close against the line of his body, and whispered, "We need to make this look good."

He pressed his lips to hers. She was lost in his embrace. His tongue stroked the crease of her lips, seeking entrance. Emma's lips parted as she gave him the entrance he sought. He pulled her closer and deepened his kiss. Her breasts crushed against the hard planes of his chest. His hands caressed the small of her back, sending tingles of awareness through her body. She didn't care who watched. She could get lost in his touch, in his strong embrace. Emma struggled to keep her wits about her, knowing he was putting on a show, but god, how she wished it were real. That it was possible to last longer than his vacation.

This is all just for show... This is all just for show.

She lightly pushed his chest and leaned out of his embrace. His smile widened in approval, successfully disarming her train of thought.

With her arms around his neck, she pulled him down and whispered in his ear. "You should have waited until we had an audience."

The warmth of his breath caressed her skin as he whispered his reply. "Don't worry, angel; we'll do it again. That was in case anyone was watching from the street." Jake kissed her neck, making her head roll back before pulling her tight against his body. He placed his arm around her shoulder and tucked her close to his side as they strolled into the café. Business was good for a Sunday. The café was packed. Most were her regulars, but there were a few unfamiliar faces in the crowd. The old ladies at their usual table started whispering to each other as Jake and Emma passed to the kitchen. She glanced around, taking in all of her surroundings. Her confident staff was handling their daily routine and duties.

"Hey, Helen, is everything okay?"

"We're fine here, boss. We heard about the accident. How are you feeling?"

"A little sore, but I'll live. Listen, if you notice anything unusual, anything at all, will you call me right away?"

Helen looked back at the other employees, her eyebrows pulled together. It was obvious she thought Emma's request was unusual. "What should I be looking for?"

"Just anything out of the ordinary, missing stuff, strangers lurking around outside, anything...strange. I don't care if it's something small. Just keep your eyes open."

"Sure thing." Helen shrugged her petite shoulders. "I need to get back to cooking. You need anything else?"

"Nope. I'll be in my office for just a bit if you need me."

Helen smiled knowingly as her gaze landed on Jake. "I won't let anyone disturb you. Oh, by the way, I left some phone messages on your desk."

She tossed her thanks over her shoulder as Jake escorted her by the elbow to her office, normally her sanctuary, but she realized the construction outside had started back up. Another migraine was forming, and she didn't have time to nurse it today. No, she had things to plan. She paused outside her door, forcing Jake to bump into her. Momma Mae was lounging behind her desk with her nurse-like shoes propped on the new mahogany.

"Is everything all right?" Jake asked as he poked his head around her, scanning the area.

"Yeah, sorry.' She shook her head and strolled through the door, stopping at her desk. Momma Mae disappeared and reappeared in the corner. The idea of sitting in the same chair didn't sit well with Emma. She'd done that once, trying to prove a point by ignoring the old woman. Emma had felt like she was sitting in a tub of ice, and she'd felt the freeze all the way to her bones. She'd learned her lesson that day and tried to avoid entering Momma Mae's personal space. She needed a distraction so she could find out what Momma Mae wanted today. Emma would be sick to her stomach if Momma Mae was here with another life or death warning, like the ones she had handed out the day before.

She pulled the requisition slips from the orders the Café had received and handed them to Jake. "Can you please take these to Helen, and tell her to place another order for anything she needs?"

"Sure." He walked out, leaving the door open.

"Okay, old woman, what's up?" Emma asked as she made her way around her desk to plop into her plush leather chair.

Momma Mae reappeared this time, sitting on the side of her desk. Her stern look held some concern, some kind of silent plea.

"Baby girl, you need to tell him your secrets."

"I can't. Not until we figure out who's trying to kill me. Then, maybe if he's still around, I will."

Momma Mae lifted one of her hands, and her transparent palm brushed Emma's arm. The compassion she was trying to show was sweet, but the coldness from Momma Mae's touch made her shiver. "He won't disappoint you, baby girl. You need to trust your instincts."

Momma Mae had only attempted to touch her a handful of times, twice when her parents had died and now. Emma wasn't sure why this was so crucial to the old ghost. "I'll think about it. What do you know about the person that's trying to kill me?"

"I'm afraid I can't give you the answers you're looking for. Just keep your eyes open and trust, not only in your heart but your gifts too." She vanished again.

Jake leaned against her doorframe before he walked in and sat down as she was going through her messages. She peeked up through her eyelashes. His fingers were laced behind his head, and he was flashing both of his dimples. He looked comfortable, and the twinkle in his eyes hinted he was up for anything. She wanted to round the desk and crawl into his arms. The thought scared her silly, but that kiss he had given her near the car had set her body on fire, and he was the only one that could extinguish the flames growing inside.

She abruptly stood. "Okay, nothing else to do here. I'm ready to head to my house."

Kate Allenton

CHAPTER 15

Jake followed her out, sticking close to her. The drive to her house was uneventful. Thank god. No cars followed them, and no one suspicious lurked outside. No internal warnings assaulted her body. Jake had her stay put in the car while he checked out the house to make sure it was safe. Reappearing a few minutes later at her car door, he escorted her inside, not leaving her side until she was safely ensconced behind the lock of her door. His persistence about sticking by her side would've been humorous if there hadn't already been two attempts on her life.

Emma set her keys on the table and headed to her room to pack some things. Grabbing a suitcase, she started filling it with extra clothes and toiletries and even grabbed her pretty underwear. *Just in case.* Jake stood watch from the door and smiled when she took things out of her panty drawer. She felt the heat in her cheeks under his blatant approval. Emma kept scanning her bedroom to see if anything was out of place before she turned out the light and walked back toward the kitchen.

She noticed her message light blinking and set her things down. She hit play on her way to the fridge to grab them both a drink.

There were the obvious two messages from her sisters demanding Emma call them back. *They must have met their babysitters.* She chuckled. One from her nephew, John, asking if she was all right, one from Ben saying he needed to talk, and then a voice she didn't recognize.

"Mrs. Bennett, we need to cancel your hair appointment with Vivian. She didn't show up today and hasn't called in, which is unlike her. If you'd like someone else to do your hair just give us a call back, and we will fit you in. We apologize for the inconvenience." *Click.*

Emma stood motionless and stared at the machine. After shaking her head, she spun on her heels toward Jake.

"We need to go find her."

"What's the big deal? Maybe she just took the day off?"

"You don't understand. I told her to leave the slime ball she was living with, and he hit her. She had a black eye, and she was scared."

Jake tilted his head. "Why did you tell her to leave him? Had you noticed other bruises before?"

She gulped her drink to buy her some time. "I had a gut feeling she needed to get away." Emma heard her voice. It was laced with uncertainty, mostly because she wondered if he would just take it at her word.

"And she left him because of your gut feeling? Had you ever met the man before?"

Emma put her hands on her hips and lifted her chin. "No, Vivian always came to my house or met me when we got together. Come to think of it, I don't even know where she lives." *Some friend I am.* Emma frowned. "But I was right. He hit her when she left.

She's staying at her sister's until he moves out."

"Did the guy know you're the one that told her to leave? Might explain why someone is trying to hurt you."

"I don't know," she whispered as she walked to the phone and picked it up. She called the salon back, but they wouldn't give her Vivian's address. Jake pulled his cell phone out and hit speed dial. His conversation was short. He stopped once during mid sentence and asked her what Vivian's last name was.

"I need a local address for Vivian Drake. Call me back when you have it."

Jake grabbed her suitcase and hurried her out of the house and to the car.

"Wait…wait. Take me back to the café," she demanded.

"Why? I thought you were done there."

"Jake, please just take me back," she pleaded.

The ride back to the café seemed to take a lot longer than it had when they first left. Jake parked the car, and Emma jumped out, leaving Jake to catch up as she made her way through the tables to the old ladies sitting in the back. She pulled up a chair just as Jake approached with his arms folded across his chest. Probably unhappy about her not waiting for the all-clear.

Mrs. Anderson was a lovely little woman and had lived in town her whole life. There hadn't been a time Emma could remember when Mrs. Anderson wasn't nearby in everyone's business. It was times like this she was glad the old woman knew so much.

"Mrs. Anderson, I need your help."

"Sure, dear, what do you need?"

"I need Vivian's address, please."

"Oh, dear, is that all? That's an easy one. She lives right next to me on Cherry Street, the second to the last house on the left, although I haven't seen her home lately. That no-good boyfriend of hers has been keeping me up at night with his loud music and no-good friends."

"I'm sorry to hear that, Mrs. Anderson." Emma grabbed a napkin and pen from a waitress walking by and jotted down her cell number. She handed it to the little old lady and asked her to call if she saw Vivian or her boyfriend again. Emma didn't even know what he looked like. She turned around at the last minute and asked his description.

"Oh, dear, well, my eyesight isn't what it used to be. But kind of reminds me of that bald cleaning guy on the commercials, except his eyes are so dark they look black."

Jake stopped and picked up Mrs. Anderson's hand. He introduced himself and placed a kiss on her knuckles. The old lady's cheek turned a shade of red tomatoes. He took the napkin from her hand and wrote his cell number on it too.

"It's a pleasure to meet you, Mrs. A. Please call me if he shows up or gives you any more trouble."

Emma rolled her eyes as she said her goodbye and walked out the door. Just as Jake got in the SUV and shut his door, his cell phone rang.

"You're too late. I've already got it. She lives on Cherry Street." Jake was silent listening to the person on the other end, then he finally said, "Emma got it for me. Meet me at that address. I'm going to leave her with you while I go check out the house."

Before he could flip the phone closed, Emma had her hands on her hips glaring at him. "Who were you taking to?"

"Jacobs," Jake said without even glancing her way.

"You don't even know what Vivian looks like. If she's there, you'll scare the crap out of her."

She sat back in her seat, staring out the window as he drove. She was silent for the five-minute drive until they parked down the block.

"Wait, isn't Jacobs supposed to be shadowing John around?" Alarm rippled along her spine as another terrifying thought slipped into her mind. What if the psycho got a hold of her nephew? She was going to kill the bastard or die trying.

"Abby said he was going to visit some friends out of town before starting a late semester at college. She can't reach him on his cell to find out which stop he's at this week. I think she has someone at her work looking into it" His hand reached for hers. "We'll find him and make sure he stays safe. I want you to stay in the SUV with the doors locked while we take a look around."

"That defeats the purpose of bringing me. If she's in there, she won't know who you are. She'll probably think you're one of his friends."

He turned in his seat with his body facing hers and gently cupped her cheek. "You aren't coming with me. I don't want anything to happen to you. Jacobs will be here in a couple of minutes. If this guy is the one trying to kill you, I can't in good conscious make you an easy target for him."

Emma knew he was concerned. She could imagine Mike screaming if he ever found out she wasn't just going to sit it out. But she wouldn't. Not if her friend needed her. There wasn't anyone that could stop her. She wasn't stupid. She knew the necessary precautions to stay safe. Staying in the car just wasn't one of them. She placed her hand over his resting on her face. "Do you have your gun?"

"Yeah, why?"

"Do you have an extra?" She batted her lashes, as if that would help convince him.

"I'm not giving you my gun, Emma. Just because you own one doesn't mean you know how to shoot it. You'd end up shooting your own foot or, worse, mine."

Emma snatched her hand off his and flipped open her cell. When Mike answered, she said, "Tell him that I can shoot a gun, and that I don't own them because I think they're pretty." She hit the speaker button.

"Hello?" He gave her a sideways glance.

"Jake, she knows how to shoot. If she wants a gun, give one to her. I taught her myself, and she's a better shot than you. She keeps a gun in her house and car for protection."

"From what?" His ocean blue eyes turned on her.

"It's none of your business," she said.

"I don't know. She's carried it ever since she was old enough to do it legally. I think it has to do with the lunatic that shot our dad."

Emma could see Jake weighing his options. She didn't want him telling Mike why she needed the gun or she'd have another fight on her hands. Emma said, "Hanging up now", and she clamped her phone shut.

"Now, do you have an extra gun or not?" She held out her hand palm up, waiting for him to fill it. Emma raised her left eyebrow. She wasn't letting him leave the SUV without her. He was either going to give her one, or he wasn't going anywhere.

"Look at it this way, if you don't give me a gun, I'll get one from Jacobs, and I'm not staying in the SUV when my friend may need me."

He gave her a skeptical look and unlocked the glove box, took out a Glock, and checked to ensure there was a round in the chamber. He checked the clip before handing it to her with the safety on. She put it in her purse and opened the door as Jacobs pulled up behind them, still in the same black business suit.

The man was sexy. Unfortunately, he stuck out like a sore thumb in this neighborhood, wearing his black business suit. The street was peaceful with little activity except for a few kids in their yards and an older man cutting his grass. Jake grabbed Emma's hand, crushing it in his as he pulled her down the street toward the house next to Mrs. Anderson's. His hold was possessive as he walked in front of her, blocking her from any danger that might jump out at them. Not many men would go up against her and try putting her in her place, but she liked it when Jake staked his claim. She glanced up at the back of his head as he dragged her behind him and then behind her as Jacobs brought up the rear. He grinned as his gaze traveled up her body, finally locking on her eyes. He raised his eyebrows in question, silently asking if she were interested. Emma shook her head and rolled her eyes before turning back toward Jake again and stepping closer to his side.

Jake's phone rang while they were still three houses away from where she remembered Mrs. A lived.

He stopped midstride and hit the speaker. "Hello."

"Hello, dear, this is Mrs. Anderson."

"What can I do for you, Mrs. A? Is everything all right?"

"Oh yes, dear, but you told me to call you when I saw Vivian's boyfriend again, and well, he's here at the café."

"Thank you, Mrs. A…. oh, Mrs. A?"

"Yes, dear."

"Stay away from him. He's a bad man."

"Will do," she said as she disconnected the call.

Jacobs looked from Emma to Jake. "I'll go check out the café while you two dig around here." He glanced back over his shoulder after he turned to leave. "Emma, keep him out of trouble."

"I knew it. I knew from the moment I met you that you were trouble," she said playfully as she started to walk again.

"Oh please. This is coming from the woman who was chased by a giant and almost killed in the car accident."

"It all started when you came to town," she said as she smiled and started up the sidewalk to ring the doorbell.

CHAPTER 16

There was no response to the doorbell, and no sounds came from inside the tiny house. She was moving around the house, peeking through windows in the back, when she saw Vivian through the partially closed blinds, lying on the floor on her side, her arms and legs bound with rope to a chair and tape over her mouth.

"Jake," she gasped and grabbed his arm.

He peeked through the same window and grabbed a gun from his leg holster.

"Stay here and call Mike."

She pulled her phone and hit speed dial. Jake kicked the back door open with his weapon drawn.

Mike answered on the third ring. "Bennett."

"Mike, thank god you answered. We're at Vivian Drake's house on Cherry Street. You need to send an ambulance and get here fast. We found her bound and gagged in her house."

"Are you okay?"

"Yeah, Jake's inside checking out the house, but my spidey senses aren't flaring, so I think we're alone. Mrs. Anderson called and said the creep is at the café. Jacobs is on his way to check it out while we check out the house."

"I'm on my way and sending an ambulance. I'll be there in ten minutes."

"Please send someone to the café."

"I'm already on it. Em, get your gun out and keep it out until I show up. If anyone threatens you, or if he comes back, you shoot to kill. Do you hear me?"

"Yeah, just get here."

She flipped her phone closed, grabbed the gun out of her purse, and went to help her friend. Jake had already gotten a knife from the kitchen and was walking toward her. Vivian's eyes were wide, and tears were streaking down her face. She hadn't noticed Emma yet.

"It's okay, Vivian. It's me... Emma. This man's with me, and we're trying to get you free." Vivian stilled in her fight and looked at Emma with pleading eyes. Emma took the knife from Jake and cut her loose.

She was trying to ease the tape from her mouth when Jake stood and walked toward the front window, peering out the blinds. Once Vivian was free, she threw her arms around Emma's neck and slumped in her arms.

"Thank god. How did you find me? Why are you here?" Vivian managed to ask through her uncontrollable sobs.

"They cancelled my appointment, and we couldn't have that," Emma said, making a joke in an effort to calm her friend down. It worked. Vivian let out a small laugh, and her lips held an upward tilt.

"Did Roger do this to you?"

"Yeah, we've got to get out of here before he gets back. I just came back for some of my stuff while he was gone, but I didn't get out in time." Vivian tried to stand on her own, but her legs were as wobbly as noodles. Emma grabbed her around the waist before her butt hit the ground.

"It's okay, Vivian. Jake's here, and my brother is on his way, along with an ambulance."

The sounds of sirens filtered through the open door, getting louder as they got closer to Vivian's, proving her point.

She put the gun in her purse and noticed Jake snap his phone closed. She hadn't even realized he was on the phone. Her concentration had been on Vivian.

"Was that Jacobs?" Emma asked. Her heart had fallen to the pit of her stomach when she saw her only friend so scared.

Jake kept his gaze on the street. "Yeah."

"Well, was he still there?" Emma helped Vivian to the couch and walked to his side, placing her head against his arm.

The muscles in his jaw twitched. His lips pulled in a tight line. "No, he had already left." Without looking at her, he said, "Vivian, what kind of car does he drive?"

"A 1970 Dodge Charger. It's a muscle car." She staggered up from her seated position and started inching toward the back door. "Why? Is he here?"

Jake turned to Vivian, his face blank. Emma knew he was trying not to scare her friend. "No, he was seen at Emma's café but was gone by the time my man got there."

"Oh god, he's coming back. He's going to come after me again." Vivian was stepping backward.

Vivian was wigging out. Emma blocked her path before she made it to the back door. She put her hands on her friend's face. "Look at me."

Vivian was shaking her head. Emma thought she was possibly going into shock. "No, we have to go; he's going to come back."

"Look at me," Emma said with a firm commanding tone in her voice. She needed Vivian to understand what she was telling her. "Mike will be here any minute. He will keep you safe until we find him. I promise."

What Emma said must have registered because Vivian stopped her retreat and stood straighter, wiping away the new tears that had fallen.

"Okay, Emma, I trust you. Thank god you warned me when you did. I trust you and your gut feelings with my life."

Jake walked to the front door and unlocked it as Mike, some additional cops, and EMS personnel entered and secured the area.

EMS started their assessment by checking her arms and legs and asking her questions as Mike and Jake stood off to the side, watching her as they quietly conversed.

Abby stomped in with Butch on her heels. She turned and put her hand on his chest. "You can't come in here. You'll contaminate my crime scene." Her sister was just as much *the job* as her brother. Although she dealt with processing evidence, she had never been attacked like they had a few weeks ago. Emma didn't blame Abby for freezing up, and she would bet Abby wouldn't let it happen again.

Emma was proud of her baby sister; she had accomplished a lot under her circumstances. She'd studied extra hard and gotten through college. She'd graduated top of her class, majoring in forensic investigation all while raising a child, without asking for much help. John had turned out to be a great kid, and Abby was an excellent mom.

"Abby, I've already told you. Where you go, I go. You aren't getting rid of me." Butch pushed passed her, and when she turned, she noticed Jake and Emma in the room.

She yelled, "Don't touch anything!" And stomped over to Emma.

"Emma Grace Bennett, why do you have this big bully following me around?"

"I thought Mike already explained it to you." Emma's lips tilted up in a grin. Butch sure did have his hands full.

"No, Mike told me it was because of the asshole after you and said I should call you. I've been calling your house all day, and no one has answered." Abby put her hands on her hips and narrowed her eyes. She was acting like Momma Mae.

Emma turned to glare at her older brother.

"What? I gave her all the information she needs."

Emma rolled her eyes and turned back to Abby. "I'm sorry, Abby; I've been with Jake. Please just humor me and keep Butch with you until we find out who is trying to kill me."

"Fine," she said as she spun around. "But you better hurry up and figure it out before I end up hurting him."

Butch walked over and put his arm around Emma while he spoke loudly to Abby. "Why can't you be more like your big sister? She's a lot easier to get along with."

Jake doubled over laughing. "Emma put you in your place this morning, and she showed me her right hook. I think you got off easy."

"I'll switch with you. You take princess over there, and I'll take care of Emma." Butch pulled her closer to his body.

Emma's heart raced, unsure if Jake would take him up on the offer. Did she want him to take the switch? If he did, she might be able to control her reactions to him and keep her secrets hidden. No, she wanted Jake, not Butch. It was Jake's arms she felt safe in. It was Jake's smile that made her quiver, and it was Jake's touch that set her on fire.

Emma drew her brows together as she looked down. Her hand flew to cover her now gaping mouth. "I'm going to be sick," she whispered. *Oh god...I've fallen for him. Stupid, stupid, stupid.*

Butch pulled her closer to his side. "I'm not that bad, Emma. I'll be good to you." Emma knew that was true, but he wasn't where her heart was, and Jake hadn't said anything. Did he expect her to rebuff Butch?

Jake sauntered over to stand in front of her. Cupping her chin, he lifted her face to his. With half hesitation and half bewilderment, she gazed into his eyes. The look she found in the depths of his blue gaze confirmed her suspicions He liked her too.

"This one's taken; back off, Butch." He pulled his eyes from her and looked up at his friend.

Mike broke the uncomfortable silence. "They're taking Vivian to the hospital to check her out, and I'm following them there. I need to ask her some questions."

"Mike, promise me, you'll keep her safe. Put her in a safe house until we find this asshole. I've got a bad feeling about this guy."

"Do you think it's the same guy who's trying to kill you?"

EMS was escorting Vivian out of the house and to the ambulance.

"It sounds like him. I was worried about her, went with my gut feeling, and told her about *everything*." Her brother's shocked expression was clear. From across the room, even Abby stopped in the middle of collecting evidence when she heard her reply.

"You did?" he asked, probably not believing he'd heard Emma right.

"I had no choice, trust me," she said with a wink.

Mike dropped the subject and turned to leave. He patted Jake on the shoulder. "We have an APB out on his car. Keep her safe and I'll call you later if I find out any more information."

"I'm on it." Jake took hold of her hand, pulling her toward the door. "We're leaving," he said to Butch in passing.

"I'm calling you later on your cell, and you better pick up. It seems we have lots to talk about," Abby said as she walked them toward the door. She drew Emma in for a hug before Jake pulled her out the door.

CHAPTER 17

Jake and Emma got in the SUV and sat in silence until he put the car in drive. Emma knew things had now changed. Somehow, he had torn through the wall she'd erected around her heart. This is the man she wanted, the one she trusted, but could she trust him with her secrets? It was all giving her a headache.

"Where we headed now?" she asked.

"Back to my place. I need to see what I can come up with on Roger."

"Mrs. Anderson's description sure fits him."

"I'm not sure, but it's the first thing I'll ask the asshole when I find him." Jake grabbed her hand and squeezed.

Emma was quiet the entire trip back. She glanced his way a few times and noticed him watching the rearview mirror and the vehicles around him. She rubbed her shoulder to relieve the knots she felt forming, but it didn't seem to help.

"You can relax in a bath while I'm researching our friend."

"That sounds great." Emma's mind had been working overtime. "Thanks again for helping me," she said shyly.

They arrived at his house. Jake carried her suitcase in, and all was quiet. Emma followed Jake to the kitchen, dropped her purse on the table, and plopped down in a chair as Jake went to the fridge and pulled her out a water bottle. She was a bundle of nerves. Someone was trying to kill her, and she didn't know what to do about Jake. She pushed the latter of her two problems to the back of her mind to analyze later. Maybe when she was out of danger, she would get a grip on her feelings.

"Prop your feet up and I'll go start your bath," Jake said as he ran his hand across her shoulder when leaving the kitchen. The light intimate touch was reassuring. Emma's emotions hung on a thread, the last thread bound to break soon. His sweet gestures and the care he showed her were breaking her resolve. She had enough in her head with the battle to figure him out to give her a migraine. She trusted him with her life. Could she trust him her secret and leave herself open for possibly one of the greatest hurts of her life?

Momma Mae appeared in the seat next to her. "You have to learn to trust again, baby girl. Not all men are going to hurt you like it did when your daddy died."

"Can I really trust him, Momma?"

"Any new venture is hard, baby girl. Learn to trust your instincts and they will show you the way. They are like the glow from a lighthouse, telling you which way is home."

"I'm scared."

"Emma, I won't lie to you. It's going to be hard but have faith that man will understand and love you all the more for your gifts. It goes against my rules, but when the time's right, I'll help you make him believe. I'll prove to him what you say is true."

"What are you scared of?" Emma spun in the direction of the deep voice. Jake was standing at the door. Oh god, how long had he been there, and how much of her talking to herself had he heard? She turned toward the now empty chair. Momma Mae had vanished as quickly as she appeared.

"I'm scared for my sisters." The lie flew off her tongue and out of her mouth before she could stop it. It was second nature to keep her secrets, but she didn't want to lie to Jake, not to him.

"They'll be fine, Emma. I'm going to have the guys bring them over tonight, so you can spend some time with them." He placed his hands on her shoulders and started to massage the tight muscles there. "I thought that might do you all some good."

"Thank you," Emma said for what seemed like the thousandth time. She felt vulnerable from her admittance to Momma Mae, and she didn't like it one bit.

Emma stood up and looked longingly into Jake's eyes. Would he honestly believe her and not think she was some freak? She put her arms around his waist and leaned into his chest. His strong arms came around her, and he pulled her close. Jake stroked her back in slow circles, she guessed trying to reassure her.

"It's all going to be okay, angel," he whispered in her ear.

She felt safe in the steel arms holding her. His strength and emotional support would get her through this. The light went on in her head, making her decision crystal clear. In that moment, she knew she would tell him the truth about everything. Emma wanted this man in her life. No, she *needed* him in her life, as much as she needed her next breath.

Jake leaned down and placed a kiss on top of her head. She would lay her soul bare to him and pick up the pieces where they might fall. This man was worth the effort, and she would put her heart and soul into making this work, whatever it was they had.

Jake leaned down and scooped her up in his arms. It was as if she were home when she was in his arms, giving her a peace she hadn't experienced in a long time. Emma leaned into his chest with her arms around his neck and relaxed into his embrace, letting him carry her up the stairs. The door was open to her room. He strolled in without hesitation and walked to the bed and gently laid her down. His knees at her sides, he leaned over and kissed her deeply, then he settled down on the side of her body. His hand stayed on her waist as his tongue tangled with hers, giving her time to back out and protest. None came. She untucked her shirt and pulled it over her head, taking all the guesswork out of her answer.

He placed a light kiss on her cheek and pulled back, searching her face. Looking for signs this was what she truly wanted. "Are you sure?" he asked, giving her another chance to back out.

The moment was tender. Emma had been intimate before with past boyfriends, but no other had ever felt so right.

"Yes," she said in a whispered breath. She knew her answer was for much more than just sex. More than what he wanted. She was giving him her heart for the taking, trusting that he wouldn't break it. She wasn't naïve. She knew Jake only wanted her body right now, but she hoped for so much more.

Jake's tender caresses caused Emma to tremble as a slight mewl escaped her parted lips. She'd longed for this moment since she'd met him. All her wildest fantasies were about to come to pass. Her heart beat a steady rhythm in her chest as she watched his muscular body flex above her. Jake slowly finished undressing her and stripped out of his clothes. His eyes appeared to darken under his intense stare, and a shiver ran down her naked body.

Resuming his place on the bed, he cupped her face as he gazed into her eyes and smiled. "You're beautiful."

They had been through so much together already. It was a wonder she was still alive. Too many close calls had made her realize how short life truly was, and she wanted this more than her next breath. She reached up to cup the side of his cheek.

"You have no clue what you have come to mean to me in such a short amount of time. No man has ever made me feel the things you do."

A smile curved his lips as he lowered his mouth to hers; his soft tongue traced the crease of her parted lips. She opened wider for him, and he deepened the kiss, their tongues lost in a sensual battle. The caress of his hand as his fingers ran from her thigh to her breast sent little sparks of electricity down her spine. She arched into his touch. She ran her hand over the satin sheet beneath her naked body. The coolness of the fabric helped to cool her heated flesh. The need to be closer pushed at her willpower. He kneaded the creamy white breast he held cupped in his hand. A moan escaped her lips.

His lips brushed a trail of wet, hot kisses down her neck on her exposed flesh as he descended to taste her delicate breast.

"Yes," she rasped.

"So beautiful, baby," Jake whispered. He swirled her dusty pink nipple with his tongue as his hand inched farther down the smooth length of her body. He stroked his finger through her wet folds.

"You're so wet for me, angel."

Emma grabbed his shoulders to pull him closer as his fingers played her like a fine-tuned instrument. Emma's eyes fluttered shut as the exquisite pleasure sizzled throughout her body. Every stroke increased the desire thrumming through her body. He stroked her sensitive walls in search of the spot that would send her over the edge.

"I need more, Jake, please," she begged as her breath hitched. Emma wanted this man. She wanted to give all of herself to him, secrets and all. After this, there would be no more running. They were in this together.

"Is this what you want, baby?" He pressed and swirled the tiny bundle of nerves, and his mouth moved to suckle her other breast. He pressed three fingers into her entrance, stroking faster. Her breath quickened as she bucked her body against his stroking hand, seeking release.

"Oh yes." Tiny pinpricks of light exploded behind her eyelids as the crashing waves of climax racked her body. She struggled to catch her breath as he continued stroking through her quivering walls until her body relaxed and she opened her eyes. The evidence of her pleasure coated his fingers and brought a smile to his lips.

He lifted his fingers to his mouth, his eyes closed as he sucked them clean. "You taste like heaven, baby."

Jake rose above her and settled between her open thighs. Her heart raced as she gazed into his deep blue eyes. He slid into her wet heat, each steady rocking motion seating him deeper. His jaw clenched as he thrust farther into her, seating himself to the hilt.

"Baby, you feel better than I could have ever imagined. So wet and hot."

Her heart swelled. Emma just wanted to wrap her arms around him and keep him there. Safe and close. She was his, and she'd decided to play for keeps. Her walls acclimated to his large size, and her breath caught as he pulled out to the tip and slid back home. Emma thought she'd died and gone to heaven. Her fingers stroked up his chest, and latching on to his silky brown curls, she drew his lips down to hers, needing to taste more.

"So good, baby."

"Take me, Jake." She wrapped her legs around his waist and dug her heels in. If he didn't start moving, she might just die. She tilted her pelvis, meeting him stroke for stroke.

"Harder…Faster, baby. Make me come." She would take everything he gave her. She wanted more than his hard body; she ached for his heart. Their slick bodies moved in tandem until she left his mouth and latched onto his nipple.

"That's it, baby." The sensation threw him over the top, snapping his willpower as she had planned. The raw need to possess her was etched on his face. She was writhing beneath him with each thrust. Her walls squeezed around him, as he felt the tremors start.

"Oh god, oh yes, Jake." Her body tensed beneath his, and her back arched as she screamed her release. His thrust became frenzied when she clenched under him, and his orgasm washed over him like a raging storm, soaking her with his seed.

His body collapsed, and he rolled to the side, taking her with him. She lay on his chest as their breathing slowed. He wrapped his arms around her and kissed the top of her head.

"I love you, Emma."

She raised her head and planted a kiss on his mouth.

"I love you too... Oh shit." Her hand flew to her mouth.

"Now, angel, please don't tell me you regret it already." Jake drew her tighter in his arms and rested her cheek on his chest.

She leaned up and looked in his eyes. "We didn't use protection."

CHAPTER 18

She searched his face and waited for a flinch or any sign of regret, but it never came. He stroked her back, and she rested her head again on his chest.

"It's okay, Emma. Whatever happens, we'll deal with it together. I want this to work between us."

They lay there thinking, for how long she wasn't sure. Jake's breathing had evened, and his heartbeat against her ear had slowed.

Emma couldn't sleep. She prayed he felt the same way after she told him her secret. The damn thing felt like a boulder on her chest trying to suffocate her. She wanted to kick herself for not telling him before things went further. *What's done is done. I just hope he genuinely meant he wanted to give us a chance.*

"Jake." Emma heard her voice crack.

His eyes were closed as he answered. "Yeah, angel."

She lifted her head and saw the peaceful expression on his face; he was sated. "We need to talk."

"We are talking, Emma." He lifted his head, placed a gentle kiss on her lips, and again rested his head on the pillow.

"No, I mean seriously. There's something I need to tell you."

"It's going to have to wait, Emma. The guys are going to be here soon with your sisters. I don't mind them finding us like this, but I don't want your sisters to give you a hard time. So, let's get you up and in the shower." He rose from the bed and held out his hand. She placed hers in his and let him pull her up. The muscles in her body were protesting. Her legs felt like wet noodles. He put his arms around her and pulled her flush with his body. His arousal poked her belly. Emma knew if she started up again, he would finish, whoever showed up be damned. She tried to pull away.

He didn't give an inch. "I promise we'll talk tonight after they leave," he said as he kissed the top of her head. Jake retreated into the bathroom and drained the now cooling water while turning on the shower.

"Your bath is going to have to wait until they leave. How about later I'll take a bath with you, and we can talk?"

Emma chewed her bottom lip. Maybe having Jake naked again when they finally talked would keep him from running.

"Okay."

Jake picked up his boxers and jeans laying where he had kicked them off at the end of the bed and pulled them on. He ran a hand through his mussed hair before he placed a quick peck on her cheek. He left her standing naked in the room. She waited for the regret and shame to hit her. It never came. She felt loved and cared for with him. She felt home. She wanted this feeling to last forever, and hoped that after the hard part, he would still be around. Emma sighed as she climbed into the shower to get ready for their guests.

After she cleaned up and got dressed, Emma heard voices on the way to the kitchen. Before she pushed through the door, she heard her cell ring. *Damn, I left my purse in the kitchen.* All the voices stopped.

"Hello." Jake had answered her phone. She didn't mind. She wasn't hiding anything from him. Well, at least nothing that could make a phone call, so she eavesdropped before entering.

"She's in the shower. Listen, Ben, she isn't with you anymore; she's with me, and I'd appreciate it if you quit calling her."

Emma's mouth dropped open. She shook her head and plowed through the kitchen doors.

"Give me that!" she said as she pulled the phone from his hands. "What do you want, Ben?" She would take care of this once and for all.

"We need to talk," he begged, not the same man who'd threatened everyone in his way in the hospital room. His whiney voice agitated her eardrums.

"There's nothing to talk about, Ben. We're over."

"So it is true; you're with that man."

"Yes, Jake and I are together." Collective gasps filled the air. She glanced in her sisters' direction. They both froze, their hands holding containers of oriental takeout stopping in mid-air over the bag. They were staring at her with their mouths hung open.

The men shook Jake's hand, patting him on the back. He ignored them. His huge smile reached his eyes, which he hadn't taken off of her watching her reaction. Emma rolled her eyes at the display of testosterone. "But I never cheated on you. I didn't even meet him until after I broke up with you."

The smell of Sesame chicken reminded her that she hadn't eaten since breakfast. Her stomach growled as she placed her hand over it, embarrassed by the sound. Jake walked to her sisters, took the containers out of their hands, and started making two plates.

"I see. It didn't take you long to get over me."

"Let's face it, Ben. It was only a matter of time. I don't think either one of us was happy, or you wouldn't have been cheating on me." Every word she said was true. Her feelings for Jake were genuine, filled with emotions she had never genuinely felt for Ben or anyone else for that matter.

"Well, I was calling about Vivian. I heard what happened. She came to see me earlier this month and wanted me to process a restraining order for her."

Emma turned from her pacing and made eye contact with Jake. He walked to her and rubbed her back. Gone were the dimples she loved so much; only concern showed in his eyes.

"Did you get it for her?" The whole room stopped to look. Uncomfortable from their gazes, she grabbed Jake's hand and pulled him from the room with the phone still attached to her ear.

"What's he saying?" Jake whispered.

Emma covered the phone with her hand to shush him.

"Well, I heard she was in the hospital. That ex of hers sure is a mean cuss, isn't he? He came to see me last week after she tried to kick him out, threatened to kill me if I filed the papers."

"Did you call the police?"

"Nope, I didn't have any proof."

"I'll mention it to Mike when I see him…Ben, be careful. I don't think he's playing with a full deck." Just because she wasn't dating the man didn't mean she wanted him to come to any harm. She didn't want anyone to get hurt because of her.

"Don't worry about me, Emma. Apparently you never did." Disdain dripped from his voice. It felt as though, if he could come through the line and choke her, he would have right then.

"Ben, I don't want to see you get hurt. Please call me if you see him again," she begged. "The entire station is looking for him."

"I've got to go. I have a client coming in. I'll talk to you soon." He hung up on her.

Emma replayed the whole conversation for Jake. To his credit, he didn't appear to be mad or jealous.

"Angel, I'm going to need to get some information from Mike. Why don't you come back with me in the kitchen and I'll finish making your plate? We need to get some food in you to replace the energy we burned earlier." He gave her a sheepish grin. He tugged her in the kitchen and pulled out a chair while he went about fixing the food. Abby was sitting at the head of the table, and Claire directly across from her. Emma just prayed they would wait with their questions until his friends were at least out of earshot.

She let out a breath she was holding when they started talking about their days' events. They glared at her as they relived Mike's announcements about their new babysitters. She looked over at the men. None of them seemed to be sporting any new bruises. Everything must have been fine. She replayed the last part of her conversation with Ben, only giving information pertaining to Vivian. She was saving the gory details of their breakup for when she could talk to her sisters privately.

She enjoyed their company almost as much as she would have had they been at Bernie's and eating Mexican. The only thing missing to the evening was Mike, who had called to talk to Jake. He had retreated from the room while on the phone but had returned, and his compelling blue eyes had sought her out.

"Ladies, since you're finished eating, why don't I take you to the library? You can relax and play catch up or whatever it is you girls talk about," he suggested, and it sounded like a great idea. She hopped up from her seat with her sisters behind her and followed Jake to the Library. She had yet to explore his house like she wanted to.

The library was enormous. The smell of leather and wood assaulted her nose when she walked into the room. Floor-to-ceiling cherry shelves lined the walls around two thirds of the room. An ornate cherry desk sat near the open wall. A fire had been set in the fireplace, and the couches and chairs looked like the kind a person could sink into and fall asleep. Emma was in heaven. She could easily read a book a day and, by the sheer volume, knew she'd never read them all in this lifetime. A rolling ladder attached to a track around the shelves would make the impossible to reach books accessible. Jake stood at the door watching her with a smile on his face. Every time her gaze met his, her heart ached for him again.

"I take it you like what you see, angel?"

"I'm in heaven," she said as she twirled around with her arms extended.

"I'm glad you like it, Emma." He sauntered over to her, pulled her in his arms against his chest, and planted a kiss on her lips. Heat pooled in her belly. The need to have him in her again overwhelmed her. When her sisters cleared their throats, he stepped away. She had to fight the overwhelming need to reach for him again and pull his lips to hers. *I've got to get a grip.*

"Ladies, there are drinks in the minibar sitting over in the corner, and just holler if you need anything else." He gave her one more kiss and retreated from the room, shutting the door to give them privacy or maybe to keep them corralled in one place. She didn't care which. Emma walked to the minibar, retrieved a beer, slipped her shoes off, then snuggled down into one of the couches.

Her sisters didn't waste any time with their questions. She gave them all the details about Ben. It surprised Emma that they agreed with her that she didn't love him. They'd been shocked about his cheating but knew it was nothing she had done to cause it. Emma and her sisters were closer than most siblings; their secrets had made sure of that. They were best friends who told each other everything, including the truth about what clothing made their butts look big. They had always been open with each other. They were the family she could trust with everything, and so she did.

She told them about Jake and how she felt and what they had already done. Including the detail about forgetting to use protection. Her sisters gave her hell about that one, reminding her that had been how John was conceived. Like she would ever forget. Abby's mood sobered when John's conception was brought up.

Claire scanned the walls, looking for something. Her gaze landed in the corner. Emma turned to see what she was looking at, and that was when she noticed the camera mounted on the wall.

"Have you told him what you're capable of?" Claire must have decided on caution, not using her abilities by name, in case their conversation was being monitored. She wouldn't have put it past a couple of the guys to listen in just to embarrass them.

"No. I tried, and he said that we would talk tonight after you guys leave."

"Em, if you truly love this guy, like I think you do, then you need to tell him and clear the air. Who knows? Maybe he will surprise you," Claire said. Both her sisters made a beeline to the minibar, pulling their own beers out.

"I know. I'm telling him tonight. If it doesn't go so well and he flips out, I might call one of you to come get me. It would break my heart, but I'm going to need one of you."

Abby walked to her and put her arm around Emma's shoulders. "Claire has a fundraiser to go to, but I'll keep my phone on me all night."

Emma knew her sister was as good as her word. She didn't know what she would do without them.

"So, Abby, how goes things with Butch?" Emma asked, trying to keep a straight face. The situation surrounding all of them was a tense one, but she figured, out of all of them, Abby would be the one to give the men a run for their money.

"Are you kidding me? He's an arrogant ass that keeps getting in my way. He has to keep reminding me this was what you wanted for me; otherwise, I would have tossed him out on his ass when I first met him," Abby said matter-of-factly.

"Abby, he's a good man that doesn't have to be helping me. Please play nice until I find out who's behind this," Emma begged. She didn't want to have to worry about her family while they tried to figure this out.

"I know, I know." She sighed. "Do you have any idea who's behind it?"

"If I had to guess, I'd put my money on that scumbag, Roger, after seeing what he did to Vivian. Besides, he matches the description."

"What about Ben? Do you think he's capable of something like this?" Abby asked.

Claire spoke up. "I don't think so. Think about it, Emma, if he wasn't working, he was with you or at my fundraiser. He's a big contributor to my charities."

"Claire, that doesn't mean he didn't have motive. Hell, he found time to cheat on me. Not only that, when we were on the phone, he did say that Roger came and threatened him. So he does have access to scumbags. Hell, he represents some of them. Just because he donates money doesn't make him a good man or give him morals. It could all just be for show."

Claire sat in silence as she appeared to absorb Emma's points. "Emma, you need to be careful when you're not with Jake."

"I am; I promise. I just wish I would have remembered to get my gun back from Mike. I was so worried about Vivian I ran off without it again." Her revolver was her baby. The semiautomatic she was now carrying held more bullets, but the amount of bullets wouldn't matter if she couldn't hit the broad side of a barn. She'd rather have the six-shooter she was familiar with on her.

Abby offered to get it and bring it to her the next day.

"Abby, ask Butch to get it. If this crazy guy knows where my café is, I'm pretty sure he probably already knows where I live."

"Didn't you stop there before you found Vivian?"

"Shit, I didn't think about that." Emma hadn't thought about that when she and Jake had been there earlier. She needed to remember to mention it to Jake. For all they knew, he could be outside the estate fence monitoring their every move.

"I'll have to ask Jake if he noticed a tail when we left. I didn't have any weird feelings, and Momma Mae was scarce, so I didn't think we were in danger."

"Still, Emma, he could have followed you. You might not have got any special feelings if he didn't threaten you or us."

"I'll remember that, Abby.

"Maybe I'll get some feelings as I sort through the evidence from Vivian's house," Abby said, tossing her head back and taking another gulp of her beer.

Momma Mae appeared, sitting in the chair behind the desk. "She doesn't need to, baby girl. This will all be over soon."

Emma turned toward the desk. "When?"

Claire swung around to see what Emma was staring at. "Is she here again? What is she saying?"

Momma Mae smiled and floated up to the ceiling. It was so unlike her. She was fiddling with the camera before letting herself float down.

"She said Abby didn't need to go to the trouble, that this would all be over with soon."

"Did she answer you yet? When is it going to be over?"

Momma Mae came to rest back in the chair behind the desk. "I can't tell you when, baby girl, just that it's almost over with. I can tell you that I sure do like that man of yours."

Emma stood with her hands on her hips. "Well, that doesn't help, old woman. Why can't you just tell me?"

"It's your destiny, Emma. It will all work out." Momma Mae vanished before giving her an answer that wasn't cryptic.

"Damn it," she cursed before turning back to her sisters to tell them what the old woman had said.

Kate Allenton

CHAPTER 19

Jake took Butch, Briggs, and Jacobs to his office and shut the door. He checked the security on his watch to make sure there hadn't been a breach. He turned on the nine monitors. Images of the inside of the house pulled up along with some of the surrounding grounds. He studied them to make sure nothing was out of place before he settled on the image of Emma sitting on a couch drinking her beer. Abby threw her arm around Emma, comforting her. Jake looked close to make sure she wasn't crying before he turned his gaze on Claire, who was pacing. That trait must run in the family.

"Dude, just turn on the sound, and you can quit trying to read their lips."

"You ass, I wasn't trying to read their lips. I was making sure her sisters weren't giving her a hard time."

"You're attached to this one. Is it because you gravitate toward the needy women?" Butch asked.

"She isn't needy. I recall just a few days ago you were getting mighty friendly with the tile in my kitchen when she laid your ass out." Jake beamed with pride, remembering how strong she truly was. "She's remarkable."

"Point taken, so what's the plan?"

"Give me a status update." He sat down at his desk and booted up his computer.

"Claire is the worst kind of humanitarian. She's a damn socialite. You should have assigned Jacobs to her. He fits in her world better than I do."

"That's why I didn't. It would have been too easy for him to get distracted." There had been a reason for the assignments he had passed out.

"Jacobs, have you found John?"

"Abby got a call from him, and I'm having him followed. He's worried about his mom and aunt and is on his way back. He's traveling by car, so it's going to take him a couple days to get here."

"Good, keep your man on him. Let me know when he gets into town, and we'll handle it from there."

"Do you know what he looks like?" Jake had yet to see a picture of the young man. Would he even recognize him? That had potential disaster written all of it.

"No, Abby talked to my guy and emailed him the pertinent information to his phone."

He hit speaker and dialed Mike's number from the desk phone.

"Bennett."

"How's Vivian?"

"She's fine. I've placed her with two officers in a safe house until we find the bastard."

"I need you to email me some information."

"What do you need?"

"I need Roger's last name. A picture if you've got one. I also need Ben's information, and I need you to send me a picture of John, so we won't shoot him when he shows up."

"Roger has a record, so that should be easy enough...Jake, I suggest you don't shoot my nephew. You think Emma and my sisters are a handful now, they would all go ballistic if anything happened to John. Even though he's Abby's kid, we all practically raised him, and trust me, you don't want the wrath the Bennett sisters can bring."

"I was kidding, Mike. Can you send me the info?"

"Sure, I'll send it in just a few minutes. How is she holding up?" Concern laced his voice.

"Better than a lot of woman would. I need to talk to you away from here. Can you meet me at McCallister's Pub tonight?" He needed to warn Mike what was going on between him and Emma. It wasn't just for show anymore. He was playing for keeps, and Mike had a right to know.

"Sure, you going to post someone at the house while you're gone?"

"You know it. Oh, one more thing. Do you know if Emma has surveillance video at the café?"

"Do you even have to ask? That was one of the first things I installed after the alarms."

Jake should have known better. If his sister had the chance to grow up, he would have done everything in his power to keep her safe, including house alarms, guns, it didn't matter. He'd need to thank Mike later for being such a good big brother to Emma. It would make his life much easier, not having to worry so much.

"Mrs. Anderson said Roger was there when we found Vivian. I'd like to see what he was up to."

"Sure, I'll get it before I meet you. How does midnight sound?"

"Sounds good, I'll see you then." He disconnected the call and walked back to the monitors, checking on Emma again. She was staring directly at the camera. He turned and walked back to the computer and signed in.

While pulling up Mike's email, he looked at Briggs. "I need all the information you can get me on Roger and Ben. I want to know everything from the number of shoes they have to the name of their first crush. I want to know their cars, their properties, anything owned by them or relatives. I want whatever you can find about police records. This needs to be thorough. I can't chance anything happening to her. Call in whatever favors you have to, just get me the information as soon as possible."

"You got it, boss."

After the email opened, he forwarded it to Briggs before opening the attachment.

He opened the attachment and stared at the screen. "Holy shit."

"What?" Butch, Briggs, and Jacobs asked at the same time as they walked around to see what was on the computer.

"He's the spitting image of the FBI guy we worked with a couple of months ago. What's his name?" He stared at the picture of John, trying to place the face staring back.

"You mean Sam?" Butch asked.

"Yeah, that's him. There is no way those two aren't related."

"Don't you think if they were related, he'd be here with Abby, or at least be concerned about his son?"

"I don't know, but I'll ask Emma about John's dad to see what I can find out. Everyone know what to do?"

"Yep," they all replied.

"Good, keep me informed. I'm going to put Emma to bed. Take the girls home and keep them safe. I don't need my woman getting pissed at me." He smiled and walked back to the security monitor, checking on Emma once more. The monitor was nothing but snow.

"Shit!" he exclaimed and ran from the room, drawing his weapon.

Jake threw the library doors open, and he sagged against the door. Butch, Briggs, and Jacobs had their weapons drawn as they ran into the room. The women all had jumped when he burst through the door. Emma had her hand on her chest.

"What's wrong?" Emma quickly walked to him.

"I must have a short in my monitors." His forehead was wrinkled as he looked up at the monitor. "When I was in my office, I looked up on the screen to check on you, and there was nothing but snow. I thought something was wrong.

Emma put her hand on his chest. She could feel his heart racing under her palm. She put her arms around him and whispered, "I'm fine. I'm right here, and everything is okay."

Jake put his gun in the waist of his jeans in the back and threw his arms around her, pulling her in close. He kissed the top of her head before whispering, "I think we need to go to bed." He turned his head toward her sisters. "Goodnight, ladies."

Emma felt ready to hurl. Her stomach was doing summersaults thinking about how she was going to explain all of this to Jake.

Claire stopped him before he made it to the door with Emma in his arms. "Jake, I need to say this." She paused and looked at

Emma then back at him. "Don't you dare hurt her."

"Claire, stop," Emma pleaded. "Jake and I will figure things out. I'll be fine. Everything will be fine. I promise."

"Claire, just for the record, Emma isn't a game to me; she's important."

Her sister stood there with her hands planted on her hips.

Butch broke the tension in the air as he put his hand out for Abby. "Come on, princess, it's time to get you home."

"I'm not your princess, jerk," she said, ignoring the outstretched hand as she pushed herself to her feet.

"I guess that is our cue to leave," Briggs said to Claire as he escorted her out.

Jake and Emma followed them to the door, locking it before trudging up the stairs.

CHAPTER 20

Emma collapsed on the bed. Jake pulled some PJs from her suitcase and helped her undress. He surprised her when he didn't make a move on her, just placed a chaste kiss on her lips. Emma thought he was trying to avoid the talk and sat up when he lay on the bed next to her, fully clothed.

"Emma, what do you know about John's dad?"

She looked at him with her brows drawn. He pulled her down to his chest and ran his thumb across the lines on her forehead to smooth them out.

"It's a long story."

"Please tell me."

"Why is it important?" she asked.

Jake stroked her back. "Emma, I will always be honest with you, and I'll tell you why I'm asking after you tell me the story. Please, angel. If I didn't think it might be important, I wouldn't ask."

She snuggled in for the long story. "John was conceived from a summer fling Abby's last year of high school. We were on vacation in Florida when she met Ryan."

"His name's Ryan?"

"Yeah, Ryan Douglas. Well, that was the name we knew him by. He and his dad were renting the beach house next door that summer. Abby fell in love with our handsome neighbor, eventually giving up her virginity."

"Why did you say that was the name you knew him by?"

"Well, at the time, we only had our mom. After we got back home, Abby found out she was pregnant and told our mom. My mom didn't freak like most moms would have. She tried to take care of the situation.

She took Abby back to Florida two months later to look for Ryan so Abby could tell him. Except when they got there, there was no trace of Ryan or his dad. She checked with the rental people, and they didn't know anything that we didn't already know."

"What did your mom and Abby do?"

"My mom used every available resource she had to help Abby try and find him. She contacted my dad's old partners, and they searched too. We bought the beach house, and every year we go back, hoping he shows up, that maybe there is the slightest chance she meant something to him. The bastard had given her a fake name. He single-handedly destroyed Abby's trust in all men. She won't admit it, but she never got over him."

"How long did you look?"

"I think she still looks. Douglas is a pretty common last name, but I don't think she's given up."

"So he doesn't know about John."

"No, but I swear to you, if I ever see him again, I'm going to kick his ass. Every year we went back to the beach house, Abby's heart broke a little more." Just remembering those times with Abby made Emma's heart clench. She wished there was a way to take some of the pain from her. If one of her abilities had been to do just that, she would have done it and not thought twice about it.

"That couldn't have been easy for her or your family, having a baby around when she was still a teen and the rest of you were only in your early twenties."

"My sister is resilient. Of course, we helped her as much as possible. But she put herself through college and raised a wonderful young man. She was a great mom. I'm very proud of how they both turned out." Emma paused while the images from the past went through her mind. She shook her head. "Your turn. Why do you ask?"

"I think I might know who he is."

Emma shot upright, and her heartbeat sped up. "You're kidding!"

"Well, I'm not sure until I talk to him, so please, don't say anything to Abby just yet. I don't want her to get her hopes up. If it does turn out to be him, I'll let you decide what you want to do." He pulled her back down to his chest and ran his hands through her hair.

"Jake, promise me if something should happen to me before we find out, promise me that you'll tell her if it's him." She'd never be able to live with herself if that bit of information was taken to the grave with her.

Intuition

"Emma, nothing is going to happen to you." He pressed another tender kiss on her lips.

Momma Mae appeared in the chair Jake had slept in the first night. "It's time, baby girl."

She pulled out of his embrace and got up to pace at the foot of the bed. "Jake, do you remember when I said we need to talk?"

"Come back and lie down with me and we'll talk."

"I can't. I'm too nervous to tell you what I need to. I need to move. Besides, when I'm in your arms, I lose my train of thought. And then where would we be?"

He sat up and scooted to sit at the end of the bed. "It's okay, Emma. You can tell me anything."

"I'm not sure what you'll think when I get finished." She wrung her hands before stopping in front of him.

Jake took her hands and pulled her toward him so she was standing between his legs. "It can't be that bad, baby. Just say it. Quit thinking about it and tell me."

She sat next to him and just blurted it out. "I have special gifts. Well, at least that's what my sisters and I call them."

He opened his mouth to say something then closed it again without uttering a word.

He took a deep breath. "Emma, what kind of gifts are you talking about?"

"Jake, just hear me out. I need to tell you everything all at once, or I won't get through this." Emma rose again and walked to the window.

He sat straighter. "Okay, I'm ready. Just tell me everything."

She proceeded to tell him about her intuitions. How they warned her of danger. How she had slipped up in his presence a few times. And then she dropped the bomb on him about Momma Mae.

His face was pinched, in the same fashion her third grade teacher's had been when Emma had tried to tell her. He had the same look as her teacher. He didn't believe her; she could see it in his eyes.

"Is she here right now?"

"Yep, she's sitting in that chair." She pointed to the chair by the bed. Jake looked in the direction, and Emma knew he wouldn't be able to see her. It would take a leap of faith.

"Emma, this is a little hard to believe. Maybe you hit your head harder than we thought." He stood and reached for her.

Emma backed out of his embrace, so he plopped back down on the bed. She needed to be clear.

"Jake, I'm not delusional." She looked to Momma Mae for help.

"Baby girl, tell him Jane misses him, but she's happy, and she doesn't blame him."

She looked back to Jake. "She wants me to tell you that Jane misses you, but she's happy, and she doesn't blame you." He hadn't told her about another woman. She was beginning to think he was keeping his fair share of secrets too.

Jake jumped up from the bed and pulled away from her when she tried to touch his arm. *So much for working through our problems.* He was already shutting her out.

"Jake, who's Jane?" Emma whispered.

"Why don't you ask your ghost?" he sneered.

Emma turned to Momma Mae, who said, "His sister."

"Oh my god. She was your sister." She turned accusingly toward Momma Mae. "Couldn't you have told me about a pet instead of his sister? You should have known that would freak him out," she said, talking to what Jake must see as an empty chair.

"Are you talking to her?" he asked.

"Yes, and she hasn't answered me," Emma snapped, and turned back to the empty chair.

"Baby girl, I needed to give you proof he would believe. There are a bunch of boys that have dogs named Spike. If I'd said he was fine and chasing cats, he wouldn't have believed you."

She turned toward Jake. "You had a dog named Spike that chased cats?" she asked.

"How did you know that?"

Wasn't it obvious? His brain must have quit functioning. Emma had already told him how she knew. She didn't know what to expect from trying to convince him she was telling the truth, but she would try, just for him. He was worth the effort. One way or another, she had to make him believe.

"I told you. Momma Mae just told me."

Jake looked at his watch. "Emma, I have to go meet Mike."

She approached him again, and he backed out the door. "I need time to digest all this. Please try and get some sleep and I'll check on you when I get back. I'll send someone to watch the house so you'll be safe while I'm gone."

"Jake." She took tiny steps in his direction.

"No, Emma, just get some rest." He left her standing in the room alone with nothing but her thoughts and the old ghost.

She stood there even though she heard the door close down below. *He's gone. He didn't believe me, and he left me.* A tear trickled down her face. The boulder on her chest didn't just feel heavy. It felt as if it was crushing her. She no longer felt the aches in her body from the accident. All the ache she could feel now had settled into her chest. More tears escaped her eyes as she shut them.

Momma Mae appeared next to her. "Give him time, baby girl. He'll come around."

"He left me. I trusted you and told him my secret, and he left me!" she shouted.

"You two will work through this, baby girl."

Emma let out a breath and looked around the room before turning to face Momma Mae. "Momma Mae, I believed you, I trusted you, and now I've lost him. How could you do that to me? He thinks I'm a freak. Just leave me alone. Just go, please." She closed her eyes.

Momma Mae disappeared sometime before she opened her eyes. Tears streamed down Emma's face, and she collapsed to the floor. She cried until she couldn't cry anymore. She hadn't felt so deflated since, well... since, her mother had died. Jake had left and taken a piece of her heart with him. She'd never trust the ghost again. He'd said they'd talk tomorrow, but she was sure it was just his excuse to get away from her. His lie about meeting Mike was proof of that.

Emma stood up and grabbed her suitcase and started shoving her things in it. She crossed the room to her purse on the table and pulled out her cell. She needed the only people she could trust; she wanted her sisters. She wanted to kick her own ass for trusting him. For believing he would understand. She should have known better than to put her faith in anyone other than her family. What the hell had she been thinking?

Emma called her sister. Abby picked up on the first ring and whispered, "Hello".

"Why are you whispering?" Emma asked.

"I swear Butch has supersonic hearing. Did you tell him?"

"Yeah." She let out a breath of resignation. "He thinks I'm a freak. He pulled away from me, and now he's left the house. I need you to come pick me up."

"That asshole!" she screamed. All pretense of her being discreet vanished.

"I need you to put Butch on the phone, please."

"Why? He's friends with him. How about I give him the slip and come get you by myself?"

"Abby, I'm not going to risk your life over my love life or lack of it. Please, Abby, just put him on the phone." Emma pulled the phone away from her ear as Abby yelled for Butch.

"Yeah?"

"Butch, I need a favor."

"Oh, hey, Emma, sure. What do you need?"

"I need Abby to come get me, and I want you to bring her."

"Where's Jake?"

"Butch, please. Just come get me. I need to get out of here." She closed her eyes. Every time she did, she remembered the disgust on Jake's face as he backed out the door, scared of her. Emma started sobbing.

"I'll kill him. What did he do to make you cry?" Butch shouted into the phone.

She could hear her sister in the background through the phone. "He's an ass. Now grab your keys or I'm leaving without you."

"Emma, we'll be there in ten minutes. It's still not safe so don't leave until I get there. I won't call him if you keep your ass in the house until I get there. If you open the door, all bets are off. He'll know you left, and something is wrong."

"How?"

"The alarm system is set to warn him through his watch; besides, I'm sure he's got someone watching over the house."

"How do I turn it off?" He had her trapped. She couldn't have left if she wanted to.

"I have the code. I'll turn it off when I get there and deal with the security detail. Just sit tight."

"Promise me you won't call him, Butch. I can't handle any more right now. I just want to leave. Please promise me."

"Emma, you have my word," Butch said before Abby grabbed her phone from him.

"We're on our way, Emma. He won't call Jake. You don't have to deal with that asshole anymore. Just stay in the house until we get there." The phone clicked off. Emma grabbed her things and went downstairs to wait for what seemed like the longest ten minutes of her life. Her mind replayed when they made love, his tender touches, and then she cried again. That was how Abby and Butch found her in the library. Abby ran to her and hugged her as Butch grabbed her bags. They followed him out the door to the car. She looked back one last time at the house as they drove away.

CHAPTER 21

Jake beat Mike to the restaurant. An empty glass and a bottle sat on the table. He'd tuned out the music until it became a dull noise in the background. He had already downed his scotch before Mike had even shown up and was working on a beer. He sat in a daze as he replayed the conversation he'd had with Emma. He just couldn't wrap his mind around her abilities. When she'd mentioned Jane, he had been shocked. When she said that Jane didn't blame him, it had really freaked him out. He shouldn't have left Emma. He should have called Mike to meet him at the house.

Emma was probably worried he'd left without finishing their conversation. Jake knew he should have reassured her, but his mind had gone blank. He'd said the only thing that had popped into his mind. He needed to meet Mike. Mike was ten minutes late when he walked through the door and came toward his table.

"Sorry I'm late." Mike handed the videotape and a manilla envelope to Jake before he pulled out a seat. He motioned for the waitress and waited for Mike to get his beer. He wanted to make sure Mike was relaxed when he told him what he needed to say.

"So what did you want to talk about?"

"I love your sister." Jake put up his hands with his palms out. He knew this wouldn't be easy for the guy. He could only imagine if one of his friends had done the same thing with his sister. He would have felt betrayed.

"Shit." Mike stood, ready to leave.

"Now wait just a second, Mike. That's not all, after I tell you what I did, then I'll let you kick my ass."

That stopped Mike in his tracks. He sat back down. "What the hell did you do?"

Mike grabbed Jake's shoulder and watched the events unfold in his mind. No lies or half truths. He would know the whole, unedited story, just the way he liked it.

"You slept with her, you asshole. You were supposed to be keeping her safe, and you slept with her."

"Let me guess. You have *gifts* too." He used invisible quote marks in the air.

"Yeah, you schmuck. You slept with her, and when she trusted you enough to confide her secret, how the hell do you repay her? You walked out on her. I should kick your ass now!"

"She mentioned my sister, and I freaked. What would you have done? And what about you, asshole? You've probably been able to do this trick your whole life, and you never told me."

****

Mike drained his first beer and ordered two more. He drew in a deep breath and exhaled. He didn't want to be the one to tell Emma's story, but it might help Jake understand.

"Emma told her teacher and classmates about her gift when she was little. They tormented her. Jake, she never got over it.

She keeps all people in her relationships at arm's length. She's never trusted another soul unless Momma Mae insisted. That's how it works. Whenever one of us is in danger, and I hate to tell you most times it's me, she gets symptoms that affect her. She describes it like PMS and uses that excuse when she needs to. She gets severe headaches and cramps. You are the first guy she's trusted. She must feel so betrayed. Momma Mae is another story. Emma doesn't know why she's here; she just is. Emma has accepted it like her second skin, even though she doesn't understand it."

"She said she loved me. Of course I told her I loved her first."

"You schmuck, you don't deserve her."

****

Jake banged his head down on the sticky table. "Man, what have I done?" he mumbled.

"She deserves better, Jake. Someone that loves her for who she is, all of her."

Jake looked up and into the eyes of the man he'd known for a long time and knew that this was important. He had to make Mike understand. "I'll find a way to make it up to her. I have to. Mike, I won't lose her."

"You and I have been practically brothers for a long time. So, I'm going to tell you straight up. You probably already did."

Mike's phone ran, and after checking the caller ID, he answered. "Bennett." After a few uh huhs, he said, "I know. I'm talking to Jake." He could hear a female voice over the phone and snatched the phone from Mike's hand. Before he put it to his ear, Mike said, "You don't want to do that, buddy. Trust me."

Jake ignored the advice and put the phone to his ear. "Emma."

"No, asshole. It's Abby."

"Abby, are you at my house with Emma?"

"No, dipshit." She paused. "Tell me, Jake, how were you going to keep my sister safe if you didn't even know she left your house thirty minutes ago? Huh, Sherlock?"

Jake glanced at his watch. The alarm hadn't gone off, which meant someone with the code had turned it off for her. *Butch.* "Abby, I need to talk to Emma."

"Nope, not happening. Not tonight and possibly not ever. She cried herself to sleep, no thanks to you, you jerk."

"Does Butch know about her secret?" he whispered, not sure how much he should reveal.

"No, and if you want to keep living, you better keep it that way. She trusted you, you ass, and what did you do? You left her alone in your house, and to go where? To a fucking bar!"

"Abby, I'm not going to tell him, but I need to talk to Butch. Please put Butch on the phone."

"Fine!" she screamed in his ear. "The asshole wants to talk to you."

Butch got on the phone. "What?" he snapped, foregoing the friendly hello.

"What's your problem?"

"My problem? What's *my* problem? Jake, haven't you done enough? If you're finished playing with the girl, just let her be. I don't know what happened tonight, but I know what I saw when I picked her up. You destroyed her, dude. She wasn't the feisty girl from this morning that knocked me on my ass. For heaven's sake, I had to listen to her trying to conceal her crying until she fell asleep. Don't worry, dude, I'll keep her safe. You just leave her alone."

"Sorry, bud, no can do. I love her," he said with confidence into the phone.

"Dude, you've got a funny way of showing it."

"Butch, I'm going to marry her if I can get her back. You better keep my future wife safe, or you'll answer to me." Jake clicked the phone shut and handed it back to Mike, who sat with his beer halfway to his mouth and his jaw almost touching the floor. He shook his head and put his beer down.

"I must not have heard you right, Jake. Did you just tell Butch you were going to marry my sister?"

"Yeah, I did, if she'll have me. The ass kicking is going to have to wait until I sober up tomorrow though."

"You do know what you're getting yourself into? She's stubborn, and she's strong, and she isn't going to take you back with just a light apology. You're going to have to grovel, and you deserve everything you've got coming to you, but I will give you some advice...she likes emeralds," Mike said with a grin on his face. "But I want you to remember, I'm still her big brother, and you'll have to answer to me, if you hurt her again.

"I know it isn't going to be easy," Jake said as he stood to leave. A plan was forming in his mind on how to get Emma back. He had to get her back. She was everything to him. He couldn't imagine his life without her.

"You've got your work cut out for you." Mike said as he walked with Jake to the parking lot. Sleep wasn't going to come easy to him tonight, but he hoped the alcohol would help.

CHAPTER 22

The shrill sound of a phone ringing woke Jake up. He grabbed the phone at his bedside table and put it up to his ear. "Hello."

No one responded. He looked at the damned thing and realized it was still shut. He rubbed his eyes and opened it. "Hello." His voice sounded gruff to his ears as he lay in the bed and stretched.

"Jake, were you sleeping?" Briggs asked.

"I was." Jake finished wiping the sleep out of his eyes as he climbed out of bed.

He padded his way down the long hall toward the kitchen. After the drinks he'd consumed, he was sure he would have slept harder, but he wasn't surprised he had tossed and turned so much. Jake knew why. He was worried about Emma. He was going to need copious amounts of caffeine today. He might as well go ahead and start now. He turned the coffee pot on and waited.

"Jake are you still there?"

"Yeah, sorry dude. I haven't had my coffee yet."

"I'm surprised Emma doesn't already have you up. Did she let you sleep in?" Briggs asked.

The memories of the night before slowly invaded his caffeine-deprived brain. "She left me last night."

"Do you know where she is?"

"Yeah, she's with Abby and Butch." He placed his cup under the dispenser. When it was full, he pulled his cup and replaced it with the coffee pot.

He took a sip. The hot liquid burned his mouth. "Why?"

"I got the information you wanted, and you probably need to go get her. She might be in trouble."

"What did you find out?" His brain was trying to keep up with the conversation, but when Briggs mentioned she might be in trouble, he stood up straighter, focusing all of his attention on the conversation.

"Mike told us Roger had a rap sheet. I started digging into the cases, and you'll never guess who his attorney was."

"Oh shit, it was Ben, wasn't it?" *I knew the bastard was no good.*

"Yeah, and, Jake, this guy is bad news. Ben got him off on technicalities. He was a suspect in a lot of bad shit. Not just domestic abuse but possible rape and murder."

"I have to get dressed. Text me Abby's address. Bring Claire and meet me there."

"Sure. She won't give me a hard time when I tell her what I found out."

"Hey, Briggs…I can't let anything happen to her. She's more than just special to me. I'm going to marry that woman if I have to haul her over my shoulder and carry her to the altar."

"Oh, shit. Congrats, boss."

"Thanks. Call Mike, tell him about Ben and have him meet us there."

He disconnected the call and downed the remaining coffee in his cup as he hurried to the shower. His stomach rolled, and he was unsure if it was from alcohol or nerves.

He rushed through his shower. As he sat on his bed pulling on his boots, he looked up to see an old lady with silver hair standing in his room.

"Oh shit!" He jumped to his feet. "How the hell did you get in here?" He jumped up away from the semi-transparent vision. The blood rushed from his face as he backed up against the wall. She advanced toward him, and he put his hand out to stop her. She looked harmless, but looks could be deceiving. His hand passed right through her.

"What the hell?" His mind went blank. He was trying to process what he was seeing, and he couldn't believe it.

"Jake, I'm Momma Mae." She stopped her advance. "I didn't mean to scare you. I planned on gradually letting you get used to me instead of just appearing, but Emma's in danger."

"No, she's not. She's at Abby's house with Butch."

The old ghost sat down in a chair by the window. "No, dear, she's not. She got a call early this morning and left."

"Where is she?" he demanded, but knew it was ultimately up to the ghost on whether or not she would tell him. Hell, he didn't have any way of threatening her.

"I can't tell you. I'm telling you too much already, but she needs your help. You have to hurry. He's going to kill her."

Just as suddenly as she appeared, she vanished. He ran his hand in the air in front of him then rubbed his eyes. If he hadn't already had his coffee, he would've thought he was still drunk or dreaming.

"Oh shit." He grabbed his phone and keys, hopping on one foot down the hall trying to put his other boot on as he went toward the garage.

He jumped in the SUV, threw it into drive, and hit the gas. In his haste, he almost took out the garage door before it had fully lifted.

He hit speed dial.

"Speak," Butch answered.

"Where's Emma?" Jake growled in the phone.

"She's sleeping in the spare room. Why?"

Jake took a deep breath. It wasn't going to help Emma if he was barking out orders. He needed to keep a clear head. "Please, just walk in her room and look."

"Sure, hang on." There was shuffling noise over the phone. "Jake, her room's empty. Let me check with Abby and search the house."

"Call Mike. We're going to need her cell phone records for the last twelve hours. Have Abby check her guns and garage to see if anything is missing and call me back. Tell Mike to hurry; Emma's in danger."

He clicked the phone closed and pushed the pedal to the floor. His phone rang two minutes later. He hit the speaker button.

"Emma?"

"No, it's Mike. How do you know Emma's in danger?"

"Momma Mae paid me a visit."

"Oh crap. You saw Momma Mae? She's never shown herself to us. Did she tell you where Emma is?"

"No, she said she couldn't, just that Emma was in danger, and he was going to kill her."

"Did she say who?"

"No, she did say that Emma got a call on her cell and snuck out. We need to know who called her."

"I'll meet you at Abby's in ten minutes. I should know by then. Jake, we can't let anything happen to her. Emma's the glue that keeps us together." His voice shook.

Jake's emotions were just as raw. He wouldn't lose her, not now, not after he had just found her. He broke every driving law there was to get there fast. His stomach was tied in knots as he sent up a silent plea. "Please, God, don't take her too." He hadn't prayed since he'd lost his sister, but he would for Emma. If it would keep her safe, he would do it every night for the rest of his life.

"I know, Mike. We will find her. We have to." He wasn't sure if it was Mike he was trying to convince or himself.

He clicked the phone shut and shoved it in his pocket. He skidded to a stop in front of Abby's house. The street was littered with cars parked haphazardly, his included. He jumped from the SUV and headed toward the door. He knew time was the enemy in cases like this. This wasn't the first time he'd been in this position, but it was the first time it was personal.

Abby came running out the door and grabbed his shirt. "She took my Beretta and my car. She left me a note saying she went to meet Ben at his office. He said he had information on Roger."

"Have you tried to call her?"

"Yeah. I tried to call Ben's office too, but no one answered, and I think her phone is turned off."

"Damn. Is Briggs here yet?"

"He just got here."

He grabbed Abby's shoulder and leaned down close to her face. "Abby, how good are you and Claire at shooting?"

"Mike taught us. What do you think?" Emma would kill him if he put them in danger, but he knew it was futile to try to exclude them. Emma's sisters were the definition of stubborn. They would just try to find her by themselves and might really get hurt. At least that was the logic he would use when he told Emma and Mike.

"I think it's going to take all of us to find her," he said as he entered the house.

Briggs was in the kitchen. He had several papers spread out on the island counter and a map spread open on the table.

"Talk to me, Briggs, what've we got?" he said as he approached the table, more concerned as the minutes ticked by.

"Ben has four properties." He pointed on the map as he explained. "One is a rental that's occupied. His main residence is a house on Sutter Hill; he lives there. He also has a cabin on the lake and a condo downtown near his office. He drives a 2011 Silver Mercedes. Mike has an APB on his car, Roger's vehicle, and Abby's. I've called in a few favors and have men posted at the airports, the bus stations, and all four major roads heading out of town. He isn't getting out of town with her. He has no known family in town but several influential friends from what Claire's told me."

"I don't think he would want them to know his dirty secrets. He won't call them for help. He would use thugs like Roger. What do we have on Roger?"

"Vivian broke up with him, and though it was her house, he refused to leave. He owns a Dodge Charger but no property. I already told you about his rap sheet. This guy plays dirty. We need to watch out for him." Briggs pulled out a picture of Roger from an envelope.

Abby grabbed it out of his hand. "That's him. That's the guy who chased us with a knife."

Mike hurried through the door, slamming it shut behind him as he entered the kitchen. He blurted out what they already knew. "Ben called Emma, using his cell." He confirmed the APB and that he had a unit headed to Ben's office.

"Well, we can rule out he would have kept her at his office since you have patrol headed there, and I think it's safe to rule out the rental property. That only leaves his house across town and the lake house."

Jake gazed around the room, doing a count. They needed weapons. "I brought my gun. Who else is packing?" he asked the collective group.

He knew the answer he would get from his guys and Mike, but he didn't expect the females to start pulling out weapons they had concealed under their clothes. Claire had an ankle holster with her gun in place, and they all gawked as baby sister Abby reached down her shirt between her breasts and pulled out a tiny gun. Butch leaned over to take a peek, trying to shift her shirt. "What else you got down there, Abby?" He smiled.

Abby punched his arm, which was sure to leave a bruise. "Stay focused, idiot." She removed her own ankle holster and then rolled her eyes at Butch's expression. "I also have a full gun cabinet. Who needs one?"

Jake was pacing. Abby could almost see the wheels spinning as he formulated a plan. The testosterone-filled room would generally have been too much for her, but she was worried sick about Emma, so she barely noticed it. The other Neanderthals were still staring at her little gun. Then it hit her. "Wait, I know how we can find her!"

Jake stopped in his tracks and turned to her. He crossed his arms over his chest. She could see the skepticism in his eyes. One day they would all figure out what she and her sister were capable of. "All I need is five minutes and a cell phone."

Cell phones were thrust at her from all directions. "I can call from the car; we need to leave." She replaced her tiny gun in her bra holster, reattached the ankle strap and practically ran out the door.

Jake was right behind her with the rest of them hot on their heels. "Abby, you're riding with me."

"I'm driving, Jake. It'll be safer, and I know the area better." He threw her the keys and hopped in the passenger seat.

Kate Allenton

CHAPTER 23

Abby climbed in the car, took Jake's cell he was thrusting at her, dialed a number, and hit the speaker button. A voice unfamiliar to Jake answered. "Hey, doll, I wasn't expecting to hear from you on your day off."

Jake glanced at Abby with a raised brow as he silently mouthed the word *doll*? Abby shot him an evil look then ignored him.

"Ted, I need your help. Emma is missing and in serious trouble. I'm calling in my favor."

"You, calling in a favor? Must be serious. Whatever you need, Abby, it's yours. How can I help?"

"I'm praying that her cell phone is still on, and the battery isn't dead. I need you to work your magic and triangulate her signal like you did on John's right before he called me. The guy that has her has a few properties, and we need to narrow it down. If hers is off and you can't get a hit, then try attorney Ben Johnson's number. He's local."

Jake knew what she was trying to do. He also expected the guy on the other end of the line to refuse. He knew the law, but he had his own connections to get around it. He didn't realize she did too.

"I'm on it. I'll call you back at this number in two minutes," he said then disconnected the call.

Abby glanced at Jake. "What? He's really good. If it can be done using a computer, he's my go-to guy." She turned right on Main. They were all looking for Abby's car.

His cell rang, and Abby hit the speaker.

"I've got her. I'm not sure if she's there, but both of their cells are in the same place. Are any of his properties you're looking at around the lake?"

She looked at Jake and smirked. "Yep, do me a favor, keep tracking it and call me if the signal moves."

Abby stepped on the gas as she headed toward Ben's property on the Lake, the other cars following on her tail. He was thankful the roads weren't too busy and most of the town had already made it to work for the day.

Jake had his fist clutched and covering his heart. "Thanks, Abby," he said as he tapped his chest.

"Jake, I'm only going to tell you this once, so listen up. If you hurt her—"

"Abby, I know I was an ass, but I love her and I'm not giving her up. I plan to marry her." He'd spend the rest of his life convincing all of them if he had to.

Jake knew the guys would follow their lead. They had performed so many similar rescues he had lost count. He needed this one to go smooth. His usual calm demeanor was gone. His heart raced in his chest as he sat in silence staring out the window, running different scenarios in his head, praying to God she was okay and he could get her out of this unscathed.

****

Emma woke disoriented but kept her eyes closed. Her head throbbed, and her body ached, the intense pain centered around the usual places, her head and stomach. She felt as though someone had taken a baseball bat to her head. Her stomach cramps were intense as she lay still on a hard floor, trying to remember what danger she had managed to get into. She tried to pull the elusive events from her subconscious, but they remained just out of reach, a myriad of events her brain wouldn't let her piece together.

Her intuition screamed danger, and she struggled to remain where she was until she had a better grasp on the situation. For now, she would play possum until she had the strength to run or fight. Muffled male voices travelled to her ears. Still not sure if she was alone, she dared not open her eyes until she was certain. She saw Jake's face in her mind. She'd been stupid for leaving him. She should have given him a chance to come to grips with her gifts.

She had expected too much too soon, but she wasn't giving up on him, not if she made it out of this alive. Emma's heart ached, not knowing whether she would live to see him again or be able to tell him that she loved him. She pushed that sobering thought to the back of her mind. She was strong, and she needed to figure out a plan to get out of here and fast. Her dad and Mike had taught her what to do. Observe, analyze, and execute. She repeated their drill in her head.

She didn't know how long she had been lying there when the events of the month started to unfold in her mind. She knew she was lucky to have survived possible death twice and didn't want to tempt fate with a third time. She tuned into her senses for information. There was a draft where she lay, and she was glad she had put on a sweater over her long-sleeve shirt. At least it helped with the chill running over her body. She took in a deep breath.

The smell of stinky fish assaulted her nose as she held back her gag reflex. Her heart sank to the pit of her stomach. The trees that scraped against the window and the fishy smell had her mind racing to determine where she might be. *Not in the city.*

The last memory she had was of Ben. He had called her and sounded worried. He had told her that he knew where Roger was and wanted her to go to the police with him. She wanted to bang her head against the floor for believing his lie. She remembered walking into his office. He'd had a stupid grin on his face before her head exploded in pain, and her world faded to black.

Momma Mae's voice startled her, but she held back her gasp of surprise, not wanting to let her captors in on her deceit. The sound of Momma's voice offered her comfort even though Momma Mae wouldn't be able to help her.

"Baby girl, you can open your eyes. They're in the other room and can't see you."

Emma opened her eyes to slits, cautious of her surroundings. Her thoughts were cloudy, and the glare from the sunlight streaming in through the window hurt her eyes. *Hot damn, there's a window. Now that's something I can work with.* She made a mental note to check if that was a viable option of escape. The room started to spin as Emma sat up slowly and blinked in rapid succession to gain her bearings.

Her throat was dry as she swallowed the moan that threatened to escape. When the dizziness passed, she used all the strength she had to push herself up to a standing position. She didn't want to be vulnerable on the floor if they happened to come back in for her. The room was bare. Just an empty closet, nothing she could use as a weapon. Emma scanned the area for her purse. If she could just find her purse, she would at least have a gun. It wasn't in sight. Her shoulders slumped.

She whispered to Momma Mae, not wanting her captures to hear. "How many?"

"Two."

"Shit," she whispered.

She was glad she had left a note for Abby. She knew her sisters would find her.

"Emma, your man is coming for you."

Emma thought back to how she had left things with Jake. "Momma, if I don't make it out of this, please find a way to tell him I loved him."

"Baby girl, your man has already met me. How do you think they found out you were missing?"

Her eyes opened wide, and her mouth fell open. Had the old lady actually shown herself to Jake? Emma closed her mouth and smiled. She would have loved to have been a fly on the wall when that happened.

"How?" she whispered.

"Now, Emma, you're smarter than that. I materialized in front of him and told Jake that he needed to find you. I promised you I would help you prove it to him when the time came for him to understand, and I did. I kept my promise."

Emma wanted to throw her arms around the ghost. Emma didn't think Momma Mae had realized the importance of what she'd done, but Emma did. Emma had more questions for Momma but knew she'd need to wait for a better time to get the details.

Emma scurried to the window and couldn't believe her luck. *What morons to leave me alone with a way to escape.* She checked to make sure it wasn't nailed in place. She scanned the creases to make sure the paint wouldn't hinder her from trying to pry it open. The sun was high in the sky and glared on the lake that stood in the distance. At least she knew where she was.

Ecstatic she could use the window as a way to escape, she shifted the lever to unlock it and quietly raised the glass. There wasn't a screen to deal with so she shimmied her way out, careful of the bush outside. With her luck, it was bound to have poison ivy or thorns.

After the successful climb, she was ready to do the happy dance but decided it could wait. Ben might be a good attorney, but he sucked at this kidnapping stuff. Her heart raced as adrenaline pumped through her veins, which worked to stave off her stomach pains. She crouched low, scanning the area to figure out the best way to run.

CHAPTER 24

Jake watched from the back of the house in fascination as Emma climbed through the window. It had taken them extra time for the short hike so they would have the element of surprise. Jake gave the hand signal for everyone to stop.

"Come on, Emma, you need to run," he whispered.

She had started her sprint toward the woods for cover when a huge bald man came at her from the front of the house and tackled her from the side. *Ahh, this must be Roger.* Jake wanted to charge the man but knew he needed to keep hidden if he was going to get her out alive. His team had the house surrounded. No one was leaving here without them knowing it. He wasn't sure how the other men were able to keep her sisters quiet as he watched the scene unfold. He was surprised none of them had rushed out of hiding.

The giant grabbed her off the ground and started to pull her back to the front of the cabin. They rounded the corner out of his sight, and Jake inched closer. He was squatted at the corner of the house as he plotted his next move. Emma came up swinging. Her right hook made contact with a bone-crushing hit to the nose. Roger backhanded her across the face without ever losing his hold and kept dragging her in the direction of the front door.

"Oh, asshole, you're going to pay for that one," Jake whispered into the wind.

Ben came running out the door after he realized he had lost their hostage and stopped short when he saw Roger had her. Jake inched even closer, not liking the odds. If they noticed him before he was ready, they would kill her. He was sure of it. Ben had his fingers wrapped around what looked to be Abby's Beretta. He held it in a relaxed grip, aimed at the ground as Emma struggled to escape the giant holding her.

Jake gave the hand signal for the teams to get into position. All he had to do was get close enough to get her out of the way, and everyone else would take the bastards out.

Jake watched as Ben walked off the porch and backhanded her across her face. "You stupid slut! Did you think you would get away? We're not through with you yet."

"Why are you doing this?" Emma asked.

"Did you think you could just walk away from me because you decided we were through? You don't get to decide; I do and don't think I forgot the asshole from the hospital either. When I'm done with you, he'll get what's coming to him. Did you already fuck him, Emma?"

"I never cheated on you, you asshole. You cheated on me." She spat, the blood from her busted lip mixing with her saliva.

"You aren't going anywhere!" he yelled as he punched her in the gut. All of the air in her lungs escaped from the force of the blow. Pain radiated through her body as she fell to her knees on the grass and struggled to pull oxygen into her lungs.

"That's right, Emma, get used to the view. You're going to be on your knees begging me to kill you before I'm done with you."

Movement at the side of the house caught Emma's attention. Jake. He was here for her, just like Momma Mae had said. She drew in a deep breath after several moments on the ground. She needed to keep the attention on her to give him a shot. She needed to try and get away from these bastards. Jake looked ready to kill. His muscles were tense, and he had his gun drawn.

"You stupid prick, my sisters will come looking for me. You won't get away with this."

"Don't be so sure about that. After Roger calls Claire for your ransom and we get our money, it's going to be months before they find what's left of your body."

Emma formulated a plan in her head and hoped that Jake would catch on. She pushed herself off the ground. "This is all about fucking money? Oh come on, Ben, Claire isn't going to fall for that shit, especially after I already told her that you cheated on me. How gullible do you think she is? And if I know Abby, I would say you probably have about fifteen minutes before she comes up here with her guns, shooting. You do know how smart she is, right? Besides, their money is tied up in accounts so they won't be able to get it for you."

She was pissing him off and stalling in case Jake needed more time. She was also getting into the position she would need to execute her plan. She stepped to the side to get ready.

"Your boyfriend will. You did know he was loaded, didn't you?" he spat out. "How do you think he's going to like your bruised and used dead body? I'm going to leave it especially for him to find. Hell, Emma, they don't even know I'm involved. They're still looking for him," Ben said as he waved his gun toward Roger.

She looked at the bald guy standing a step behind her. She was judging the distance she had. "You're the asshole who chased me and beat up Vivian."

"Yep, that's Roger, you stupid bitch. I would say he's pretty pissed at you too. I might not get months to play with you before he kills you."

"You screwed up, baldy. Vivian is my friend."

Emma brought her knee up into his groin as hard as she could. As he doubled over in pain, she sent her palm up, smashing it into his face and breaking his nose. He cupped his nose and went down screaming. "Kill that bitch!"

Time seemed to pass in slow motion. She pulled the gun she saw in the waistband of his pants as he was bent over. She spun with the gun in her hand at the same moment Ben lifted the gun and pointed it at her. Jake rushed toward her as she and Ben aimed at each other and squeezed the triggers. No one needed to get hurt because of her.

Jake landed on top of her. The air burst from her lungs at the impact, then she struggled to breathe with Jake's big body on top of her, smothering her. Gunfire erupted from the trees, the bullets flying in their direction.

Jake used his body to shield her from any stray shots. She needed to shield him. She couldn't lose him. Without a doubt it would kill her.

She tried to turn her head towards her abductors to see if they were down, but Jake stopped her. He held her face with his palms. "I love you, Emma," he whispered before he slumped to the side and his eyes closed.

"Jake!" she screamed. She saw blood on his shirt. She snatched off her sweater and ripped his shirt open to find the bullet hole. She applied pressure to his wound as she cradled his head. Tears streamed down her face.

"No, baby, not like this, not now." She shook him. "Wake up, Jake, I need you. Wake up." She wasn't going to survive the pain if she lost him. It felt as if someone had torn her heart clear out of her chest. This wasn't happening, not again. Not someone else she loved.

"Someone call an ambulance!" she screamed. Fear overwhelmed her.

She felt arms pulling her away from his body, but she struggled to get back to him. Her fist connected with someone's flesh. Her brother was holding her arms, turning her into his embrace so she couldn't see Jake. "What the hell are you doing, Mike? He needs me, let me go."

He turned her loose, and she returned to Jake, lifting his head. She could hear the sirens in the distance and knew that help was on the way. Tears dropped on his face as Emma placed a kiss on his lips. "I love you," she whispered.

The clearing was now bombarded with cops and emergency personnel. Hands were on Emma once more, this time moving her gently while they checked Jake's vitals before moving him to the ambulance. She climbed into the ambulance behind them, and the vehicle took off with the sirens blaring. She watched with hope as the EMTs worked their magic.

Kate Allenton

CHAPTER 25

Jake woke up disoriented. He looked around the room and found Dr. Lister writing on a chart.

"Welcome back," she said, putting the chart on the table.

"Dr. Lister?" Jake asked.

"That's a good sign. You know who I am."

"Where's Emma?" he asked as he tried to push himself upright in the bed.

Emma rushed over and placed a hand on his shoulder, pressing him back down onto the bed. Tears stained her face, and she was still wearing the same clothes from the lake house. She sat on the bed next to him and leaned forward, placing a kiss on his lips. "You scared me."

"I'm sorry, baby." He kissed her back.

His throat was so dry the words came out raspy. Dr. Lister took the cup from the table and handed it to him. The cool liquid slid down his throat as he took small sips.

Jake's memories came crashing back. Emma was safe. *She's alive, and she's safe.* Emma wiped the tears that escaped her eyes.

"Aw, angel, what's wrong?" Jake grabbed her hand and squeezed.

"I thought you were dead. I thought I'd lost you. Don't you ever do that to me again," she said, scolding him.

The doctor made a silent retreat from the room, giving them privacy.

"I'm so sorry, Jake; it's all my fault." More tears slid down her face.

"For what, angel?"

"For getting mad at you and leaving. If I hadn't left, you would have gone with me to meet Ben. It's my fault you were shot trying to protect me."

"Baby, I'm fine." He lifted the covers to check out his limbs. "Well, at least I think I am." He grinned. His chest was wrapped in bandages, but that seemed to be the extent of his injuries. "What happened to Ben and his thug? Please, don't tell me they got away."

"They're dead." More tears escaped her eyes. He knew she was trying to hold it together for him.

"I love you," Emma whispered as she leaned over and pressed her lips to his once more.

"Are you sure, angel?" he asked, uncertain if she knew what that meant. He wondered if the guys had told her his plan.

"Yes."

"Thank god, Emma. I want you to hear me out before you say anything."

Emma's gaze searched his before she answered. Her eyebrows drew together, and fine lines creased her face. "Okay."

Jake cleared his throat and took her hand in his. "Emma Grace Bennett, I love you with all my heart. I love everything about you, just the way you are, and I can't see my life without you in it. You are the heart I thought I'd lost. You bring sunshine into my soul, and I promise to spend the rest of my life loving and cherishing you the way you deserve if you'll let me. Emma, I would be honored if you'd agree to be my wife."

Jake thought he saw a smile underneath the hand covering her mouth. There seemed to be a twinkle in her eyes that once again brimmed with tears. He watched as they ran down her face. He hadn't wanted to make her cry again. She'd had enough of that for a lifetime. He hoped these were happy tears.

"Yes, yes, yes," she said, and pressed another kiss to his lips. "I will," she whispered, and deepened the kiss.

Momma Mae sure picked inopportune times to show herself. The apparition appeared out of thin air in the confines of Jake's small hospital room. But it wasn't Emma who noticed her first; it was Jake. Jake pulled back from the kiss.

"Emma, we seem to have a visitor."

"Everything worked out just fine, baby girl. Just like I said."

"I love you, Momma Mae. If I could hug you, I would. Thank you for telling Jake that I was in danger." Emma's annoyance toward the old ghost had vanished. Momma Mae had come through when she needed her most. She was just like family, and that was what mattered most. Emma wasn't sure if ghosts could cry, but the old woman's eyes seemed glazed with tears. "Are you sticking around or is your work here done?"

Emma had become fond of Momma Mae, even though she was a pain in the ass. She meant well, and that's all that mattered. Momma Mae had once been the bane of her existence but had somehow become her savior. She hadn't seen that one coming, but she was grateful nonetheless.

"My time here isn't over, baby girl. My family still needs me. Besides, I'm gonna have my hands full with that little bundle of joy growing in your belly. She's gonna need me too."

Emma felt a warm glow flow through her body as her hand flew to her stomach, and her gaze quickly turned to Jake. For the first time in her life, Emma didn't know what to say.

Jake's smile broadened in approval as he reached for her hand and then looked at Momma Mae. "A girl, huh?"

She turned back to the woman that, at times, seemed like her mother. "Really?"

"Yes, baby girl, really." Momma Mae moved closer to Jake's hospital bed. "Jake, your sister is so proud of you for keeping your vow twenty years ago. She thinks you deserve a medal, and since I can't give you one, I'm going to share another little secret with you." Momma Mae leaned forward and whispered loud enough for Emma to hear, "She's gonna have brothers and another sister too."

Momma Mae vanished, leaving Emma stunned. Jake's laughter filled the air, pulling her from her thoughts. "I love you, Emma."

If you enjoyed my story, please leave a comment on Amazon.

If you would like to sign up for my newsletters about upcoming releases, please go to <u>www.kateallenton.com</u>.

Enjoy an excerpt from the next book in the Bennett Sister's Saga,

A Touch of Fate:

Abby and Ryan's reunion

Available April 2012

Abby stood oblivious to the crowd behind her with her champagne in hand, staring toward the orange and red sun as it lowered beneath the horizon. She smiled. *This is what peace feels like.* Her heart felt full for the first time in years, happy for her sister and the union with the man she loved. The reception was ending, like the old chapters in her sister's life. Emma's happily ever after was just beginning with the promise of happier times yet to come. The clinking of glasses and conversations carried on behind her. Abby ignored it all, soaking in the serenity that the moment had to offer.

A gentle touch on her arm pulled her from her solitude. She inhaled a deep breath and admired the sunset once more before she plastered a smile on her face and turned to greet the awaiting wedding guest vying for her attention.

Recognition hit her like a punch in the gut. Her smile fell just like the champagne flute from her hand, now lying in broken shards on the floor. She stepped back instinctively. A ghost from her past, the one man she had searched for over the last eighteen years, stood a foot away. The same man that had altered her life forever. She felt the blood drain from her face and her world start to spin as her gaze locked with his.

"Abby, you're just as beautiful as I remember." His smile reached his eyes that glistened under the twinkling lights.

"Ryan," she whispered, unable to do more. The years barely showed; his handsome features remained unchanged. Eyes the color of sapphires stared back at her, and he wore the same smile that had stolen her heart so long ago. Her muscles tensed as she tried to push down the lump in her throat. The wall around her heart constricted and faltered for a brief moment. Her brain refused to process what he was doing here, hell, that he was actually here at all.

"I've missed you," he replied as he took a step in her direction.

The crunch of the glass beneath his shoes brought her out of her daze. Abby flinched as his hand lifted to touch her, the same hand that brought her pleasure years before now brought a cold chill. Her feet froze in place, making her unable to flee. She shook her head in disbelief as she tried to regain her composure. No, she wouldn't let this man get to her, not again.

She wasn't the same naive girl from before and hadn't been in a long time. Becoming a mother had remedied that. He didn't even know her anymore, and he'd

Kate Allenton

never known his son. Abby had imagined this moment for the last eighteen years of her life, yet no words slipped past her lips.

This man was a stranger and a liar. Angry tears threatened to fall. She clenched her fist tight, digging her nails into her palms. Her blood boiled at all the lost years she would never get back crying over the one man who had hurt her beyond repair. Why was he here? How dare he be here! Abby pulled her arm back with her clenched fist and swung, hitting her intended target. His head jerked to the side, unprepared for her reaction.

She let out a breath and rubbed her throbbing hand, pain radiating up her arm. She didn't drop him on his ass as she had planned all those years ago, but an instant red mark appeared, satisfying the anger she felt inside. "Abby, please let me explain." He held his hand out to her in a silent plea.

"You lost your chance eighteen years ago, Ryan, or whatever the hell your real name is."

She turned took two steps and paused, spinning around to face him once more. "Go to hell, Ryan!" She stomped off in search of her sisters. Abby's unshed tears threatened to fall as her heart threatened to beat out of her chest. *This isn't happening.*

There was no way in hell she was ever going to forgive that man.

ABOUT THE AUTHOR

Kate has lived in Florida for most of her entire life. She enjoys a quiet life with her husband and two kids.

Kate has pulled all-nighters finishing her favorite books and also writing them. She says she'll sleep when she's dead or when her muse stops singing off key.

She loves creating worlds full of suspense, secrets, hunky men, kick ass heroines, steamy sex and oh yeah the love of a lifetime. Not to mention an occasional ghost and other supernatural talents thrown into the mix.